Jane Digby's

Diary

Fill your paper with the breathings of your heart.

William Wordsworth

1873

Damascus, Syria
June 22

I make public this account of my life knowing that if I
do not my life will be subject to the subtle
manipulations and outright lies of the most egregious
mode of manipulations known - the tabloids. Not many
women live to read their own obituaries, but it was my
grave misfortune to do so. I am not superstitious and
no newspaper can kill me before my appointed time,
but I am truly distressed by the great fiction spun by
The Morning Post and perpetuated by others. My
"remarkable career" was recounted with such disdain
for the facts but with such conviction that my family
and friends in London became understandably

alarmed. I received so many anxious letters that I have spent weeks responding to them, assuring those I hold dear that the reports of my death, and the absurd retrospects of my life, were fabrications of the meanest kind. I now realize that publishing a true account of my life is the surest way to prevent such fictions.

For nearly fifty years I have kept a diary where I have recorded truths more rebellious and more scandalous than any scandalmonger could understand. I have lived a life I chose - and the life I choose. Can many women make that claim? We women are taught to obey the commands of a society little concerned with our happiness. We must find satisfaction in home and family - and if home and family prove not enough? Well, a fashionable woman might sin, as long as she is discreet.

And I have sinned, but indiscretion is my worst sin. My lovers have included a lord, a prince, a baron, and kings. Brigands and Bedouins have courted me. I have travelled from England to France, from Switzerland to Austria, from Germany and Italy to Greece, only to find my heart and my true home in the Syrian desert. I have sacrificed all without regret to one great and absorbing passion, the need to love and be loved.

Judge me - or not - by my own words.

Volume One:

To

Begin, Begin

1824

My seventeenth birthday! I am so *very* spoiled. Mama and Papa have given me my heart's desires, a metal nib pen to replace my feather quill and a lovely watercolour set and easel with lessons to come. But my favourite gift is you. My dear Steely, knowing my restless mind, thought I might need a secret place - a pretty diary with the *most* clever lock and darling key - to record my thoughts. Will you be my friend, or better still, my only sister? If so, I shall need to name you. I *simply* cannot keep calling you, *you*. How very rude.

I think I have the perfect name for you . . . Marianne. Marianne Dashwood is my favourite character in my

favourite novel, *Sense and Sensibility*. In it Miss
Dashwood has said,
"It is not time or opportunity that is to determine
intimacy - it is disposition alone."
I do so agree! Marianne, we are so much alike . . . such
secrets we will share!

April 4

My dear Marianne, I must tell you of my family and
home. Here are the PERSONAE DRAMATIS of my life:

Thomas Coke of Norfolk, or "King Coke," my seventy-
year-old grandfather and owner of Holkham Hall.
Married to twenty-year-old, Lady Anne Keppel.
Recently fathered a new "Crown Prince" of Holkham
(how scandalous!).

Rear-admiral Henry Digby, hero of Trafalgar, my father
and my darling Babou.

Jane Elizabeth Coke Digby, "La Madre" to her family,
Lady Andover to all others. Possesses second sight!

Ann Margaret Digby Anson, aunt and sister to the Janes
and mother to my eleven (yes, eleven!) cousins.

Miss Margaret Steele, or "Steely," my governess, and sister to yet another Jane, an *artiste* and my new watercolour tutoress.

George Anson, my oh-so dashing cousin, brother to Henry, my reckless friend.

Edward Digby, my most annoying brother who hates that I best him in horse racing.

Kenelm Digby, my sweet baby brother and namesake of the notorious Sir Kenelm Digby!

Although Forston House is our family's true home, Holkham Hall is where my family lives when Papa is at sea. Here Mama, Aunt Anne, my brothers, and my cousins have run of Grandpapa's estate. Holkham looks like a huge Roman palace, so huge that even the servants have lost their way in its hallways. Open air courtyards, archives with old manuscripts, and galleries with paintings and sculptures impress visitors. I though prefer its grounds. Our King has planted thousands of trees and created gardens, greenhouses, and farms in his realm. Here my brothers, cousins, and I spend sunny days. But *my* favourite spots are Holkham Lake where we swim naked in the summer and the stables where I visit my colt, Shelley, and where we all have learned to sit well on a horse.

Stormy or cold days I might hide alone in the library reading Byron, admire the latest blooms in the conservatory, or search with cousin Henry for the ghosts of Holkham who haunt its dark corners. Henry says we will be married one day, even though we are first cousins. I say nothing since his brother George is the one I secretly hope to marry one day, even though at twenty-seven he is far too old to pay attention to a seventeen-year-old. I *shall* change that!

Steely is calling. Farewell for now my new friend.

April 5

We are to tour France, Switzerland, and Italy! Papa must visit Italy as part of his duties as Rear-admiral, and dear Mama has convinced him to make it a family trip, no doubt thinking I shall not travel after I go to school for finishing. Both Miss Steeles will accompany us, though Edward and Kenelm will remain at home with their tutors, since they will go on their Grand Tours when they graduate university. I shall see the Continent before them! We will cross the channel by packet to Calais, there we travel by coach to Paris, then to Geneva and onto Florence. Mama has said that the trip across the Alps is "sooo arduous." How wonderful!

Forston House

Dorset, England

April 15

A thousand pardons, Marianne, for neglecting you. We have been so busy on our return to Forston House. Our home has been turned upside down in preparation for Europe. Trunks retrieved from cobwebbed attics are dusted. Inventories of clothes, china, and cutlery - to better anticipate our Parisian shopping needs - are made by servants under the watchful eye of La Madre. These exertions *and* the endless spring rains have caused Steely and me (or is it I? I can never remember) to be relegated to the schoolroom. She reads the novels of Mrs. Radcliffe, while she forces me to practice my piano and needlework! I loathe both. I much prefer my guitar or sketch book. Even dear Babou and his loyal dogs have retreated to the library to avoid drowning in the domestic flood of activity. In just one week we set sail!

Calais, France
April 23

We have successfully crossed the channel from Dover. The crossing was difficult for poor Mama, Steely, and Jane - but Papa and I proved good sailors despite the choppy waters. We are staying the night at *Le Chariot Royal*, and dear Babou and I dined alone, since the others are still feeling unwell. I am ashamed to admit that I delighted in having him to myself! We practiced our French over a late supper, as he explained how much Europe had suffered under Napoleon, and how only recently the Continent is safe to travel again. He did not say so - he is far too modest, Marianne - but his efforts as Rear-admiral must have helped bring about that safety! Papa also told me that the trip to Paris, by coach-and-four, takes anywhere from eighteen to twenty-four hours, depending on the road conditions. I shall pray for fair weather tomorrow.

April 24

We awoke to rain of the most persistent kind. It rained when we broke fast. It rained when we entered the hired coaches. It rained when we stopped to rest the horses. Mama complains endlessly about the inconveniences she suffers in travel. Luckily I share a coach with the Misses Steeles, while poor Papa must ride with La Madre, her maid, and his manservant. I spend the hours reading aloud Sir Walter Scott's *The Bride of Lammermoor* to Steely and Jane, writing to you, of course, and watching the French countryside.

I dream of Paris as the percussion of horseshoe, coach wheel, and raindrop lulls me to sleep.

April 25

We have been told sad news. Lord Byron has died of fever in Greece. Poor, poor man, to die alone and so far from home.

So we will go no more a-roving
So late into the night,
Though the heart be still as loving,
And the moon as bright.

For the sword outwears its sheath,
And the soul outwears the breast,
And the heart must pause to breathe,
And love itself have rest.

Though the night be made for loving.
And the day returns too soon.
Yet we'll go no more a-roving,
By the light of the moon.

By Lord Byron

Finis

Paris, France

April 26

Bonjour, Marianne. Today I awoke in Paris at the *Hotel Meurice*! After an uncomfortable night at a country inn and another hard day's travel we finally arrived at our destination. *Zut,* I hear Mama calling me for breakfast, I must fly *tout de suite.*

Pardon, Marianne, for my hasty departure. Mama and I spent much of the day shopping on *The Passage des Panoramas*, a covered walkway filled with all manner of shops and decorated with panoramic scenes of Paris, Rome, Amsterdam, and Jerusalem. Here a shopper can avoid the traffic of Paris. The walkway also has gas lighting to brighten its dark corridors. How wonderful to live in modern times! We purchased writing paper and chocolates, and after our exertions we sat for tea. Later we hired a *fiacre* to *Palais Royal* where we visited a milliner to be fitted for new bonnets, purchased beautiful paisley shawls, and ordered new porcelain dinnerware for Folston. Mama told me that after dark, the shops close. Then the theatres and all manner of improper establishments open . . . how fascinating!

April 27

Switzerland-bound Jane and I spent our

I'm afraid I am in quite a scrape, my friend. Last night I
had the regrettable idea to explore the *Palais Royal*
without La Madre. I chose as my partner in mischief
sweet Jane. Unlike Steely, her sister craves adventure,
and I convinced her that the opportunity to see the
great actress, Mademoiselle Mars, at the *Comedie
Francaise* in *Tartuffe* should not to be missed.
Unfortunately Steely, having discovered us missing and
fearing for our safety, alerted both Mama and Papa. The
scene awaiting us on our return was more dramatic
than any Moliere play. Papa paced the floor as he swore
most dreadfully. Mama cried, all the while sending both
Jane and me reproachful looks. Steely nervously wrung
her hands, no doubt believing that she might be blamed
for our misdeeds. I threw myself at their mercy,
admitting that the idea was mine alone, and that Jane
only agreed to accompany me to keep me from harm.
Our punishment? We are not to leave the hotel for the
remainder of our stay. I shall miss riding the roller
coaster at *Parc Beaujon*! But seeing the Mademoiselle
on stage was so worth the punishment. How beautiful,
how talented she is. What freedoms she must enjoy.

May 2

Dear Marianne, we are once again on the road, Switzerland-bound. Jane and I spent our Purgatory in Paris with watercolours. She has forgiven me and is teaching me the rudiments of the patient art of brush, paint, water and paper. She tells me that my sketches show promise and will serve me well when I become more proficient with the watercolours. She is *too* kind. But my feeble efforts and her encouragement spur me on. Now we face over three days of travel by carriage with a *still* unforgiving and unpleasant Steely. It is most provocative and bothersome! I shall instead think of the snow-covered Alps and the cool waters of Lake Geneva.

Geneva, Switzerland
May 6

Mama and Papa have often spoken of the beauty of the Alps, though nothing they have said prepared me for the lovely strength of their peaks. They frame the deep green treeline and azure blue of Lake Geneva so perfectly I fear trying to capture the sharp line and brilliant color on paper will only show me terribly unskilled. But I shall try with dear Jane's assistance. According to her, Lord Byron wrote of Geneva in *Childe Harold* and *Prisoner of Chillon*. And Steely tells me (yes, she is speaking to me again!) that Rousseau used it as the setting in a novel called *Julie*. I really must further my reading!

Mama says that Papa will take all four of us to tour the *Chateau de Chillon* tomorrow before he leaves for Italy a few days before us. *Geuten Abig*, my Marianne.

May 7

The weather was sunny and mild for our outing yesterday, though the Chateau de Chillon was damp, foreboding, and utterly fascinating. I cannot help but wonder how its famous occupant Francois Bonivard managed to bear his imprisonment here - lashed to a pillar for three years with no freedom, no light or love. No wonder Bryon was inspired to carve his own name on one of the prison walls in tribute to the man!

This morning we said our sad goodbyes to Papa. He kissed Mama sweetly, hugged me tight, shook hands with Steely and Jane and asked them to look after "his two beautiful girls." We will miss him so.

Florence, Italy

May 15

Apologies again for not writing for so long, Marianne. I fear steadfast correspondence is not in my character. But let me tell you the latest in the Digby family travels. We spent many long and difficult days on the road. I shared a carriage with poor Mama who suffered a bout with her sick headaches. Her maid, Cecile and I attended to her the best we could, though I am afraid neither of us had the skill or patience for such an exacting patient - neither cold compresses nor kind words helped ease her pain. You can imagine our relief when we arrived in Florence late today. Here Cecile has found the services of a doctor who administered a sleeping draught to our dear La Madre. Thank God for the services of a good lady's maid! We will all sleep well tonight. Tomorrow Florence awaits! *Arrivederci, cara.*

May 16

Ciao, Marianne. Steely, Jane, and I toured the city today with Mama's blessings, though with a stern warning to "conduct myself as a lady should." We started early to avoid the city's sultry heat. The morning light glowed golden on the white and muted brown buildings of *Firenze* as we walked along the Arno river bank from our hotel, the *St. Regis*, to our destination, the *Piazzo della Signoria*. There we found Michelangelo's *David* who stares fiercely towards goliath Rome. Jane and I agreed that he is a most beautiful rendering of masculinity, though I fear Steely disapproves. She is far too correct to appreciate his . . . unclothed form! We continued on to the *Ponte Vecchio*, an arched stone bridge lined with all manner of shops. In one I found a pretty lute with such exquisite tone. I *must* have it, though my allowance is too short of *lira*. Steely has suggested that I write Papa with a request for an advance, with her approval. I shall do just that. Dear, dear Steely, just when I think her too dull for words, she surprises me with her kindness.

May 30

Dearest Papa has finally returned from his business in Venice, and he came bearing wonderful gifts for us all! Steely and Jane received yards of wonderful Venetian lace, Mama, a striking *parure* of deep blue Venetian glass to match her lovely eyes. Even sweet Cecile and Papa's manservant, Jack, were not forgotten, as they were given bonuses for taking such good care of us all. But the sweetest gift was for me - my lute. Papa said that I wrote such a pretty letter asking for my advance that he decided to buy it for me outright! I am already learning the traditional English folk song, *I Will Give My Love an Apple.*

I will give my love an apple without e'er a core
I will give my love a house without e'er a door,
I will give my love a palace wherein he may be,
But he may unlock it without any key.

My head is the apple without e'er a core,
My mind is the house without e'er a door.
My heart is a palace wherein he may be
And he may unlock it without a key.

Are not the words beautiful, Marianne? And the music is equally so. Mama, Papa, and the Misses Steeles agree that the soft sound of the lute complements my soft voice better than the guitar or the piano. It is fortunate that they enjoy the sound, as I plan to practice faithfully during our long journey home. We leave day after next!

Paris, France

June 14

My dear Marianne, we have just arrived in Paris after a tedious but uneventful journey. We will rest for two days before completing the remainder of our tour. Tomorrow we see *The Louvre* and *Tuileries Garden*. Tonight we will sleep in feather beds! I shall dream of Forston and Holkham Hall - and of George Anson's warm brown eyes. *Bonne nuit.*

June 16

We all thought *The Louvre* rather disappointing. Papa said that much of its former collection were Napoleon's spoils of war from his campaigns in Egypt and Italy, but after Waterloo many of those spoils were taken to the British Museum, including the famous Rosetta Stone, whose hieroglyphs are now being studied by the linguist, Champollion. Since I have shown such interest in Egyptian artifacts, dear Babou has promised to take me to the British museum after we return to England. I wish that I could study and search the world for remnants of ancient civilizations - how wonderful *that* would be. We also saw Veronese's painting *Wedding at Cana* which, because of its large size, was deemed too large to return to Venice. Steely said its survival is as miraculous as "Christ's turning water into wine." Napoleon had ordered the painting burned, but that order was ignored by some of his men. Jane and I thought it very brave to ignore an order from "Boney."

The remainder of our day was spent in *Tuileries Gardens.* The cold and damp of a reluctant spring has finally made way for brilliant sunshine and for the perfume of roses. Mama said it is "*de rigueur* to promenade at the gardens." I suppose fashionable people - like the Digbys - must flaunt our British sophistication for all of Paris. How awfully absurd!

Calais, France
June 18

As I write this entry I sit looking at Dover. Its white cliffs shine bright in the morning sun. Our ferry, powered by steam rather than wind, hums with a harsh exhale as it churns the sea before it. In a few hours we will be home. For over seven weeks I have travelled the continent. England looks so much smaller now - a bit of earth adrift in cool seas. I long for my home but also dream of continued travel. I cannot imagine my future without both. I dream of hot sun and exotic locales, though I miss my animals - our menagerie of cats, dogs, birds, and my willful colt, Shelley. I also miss brother Kenelm, whose homely face and constant heart shines in my memory, like the fairer face and more fickle heart of brother, Edward. Mama and Papa have brought them many gifts, including two sets of *Battledore and Shuttlecock* and a book of codes and ciphers which I shall charm them into sharing with me. Papa also bought a John Constable cloud study in watercolour for Grandpapa's art gallery. Constable's work captures such feeling with such simplicity. I too want to express such beauty.

I fear I want too much.

Forston House

Dorset, England

June 22

Although it is good to be home, I am greeted by bad
news. My sweet boy, Shelley, is ill. Grandpapa has
looked at him to see what can be done. Sadly he deems
the sickness, the strangles, and advises we separate the
colt from our other horses here at Forston, as the
disease may spread. William, one of our young grooms,
volunteered to nurse him. I find myself at the stables
every moment I can spare. Poor Shelley's neck is
swollen, and he is having difficulty breathing. We fear
he may not survive. I am praying very hard, Marianne.

June 23

Shelley died early this morning.

I crept out of the house late last night to find William
tending Shelley the best he could, though the swelling
was far worse and his breathing so difficult to hear -
even his flesh was hot to the touch. My dear colt took

his last breath with his head cradled in my lap. William held me as I cried.

I have never seen death before.

June 24

I again stand accused of wild and willful behaviour. La Madre tells me my behaviour last night was "unbecoming to my social standing" and that proper young ladies do not "steal away in the night" for any reason and "leave themselves vulnerable to servant gossip." Even Shelley's death did nothing to soften her anger. I am to leave for the Seminary for Young Ladies at Tunbridge Wells as soon as can be arranged, and William is to be dismissed. I pleaded to Papa to keep William on, and he has agreed to allow his transfer to the stables at Holkham, but we are never to speak again. Evidently the head groom saw our "inappropriate" behaviour and reported it early this morning.

Oh Marianne, it is all so unfair! We did nothing wrong. My heart is broken, and appearances are all she sees.

June 25

I find unlikely allies in this domestic crisis. Edward and Kenelm have agreed to write me at seminary . . . in code. In preparation we have poured over the book of ciphers Papa gave them and selected one which we will use for our secret *communique*. Our plot is a welcome distraction from the awful death of my darling colt and the cold relations here at Folston.

June 30

My last day at Forston before my banishment to Tunbridge Wells.

Steely has revealed the true reason for my mother's anger and worry. Mama foresaw my future in a dream, one in which I am alone and lost in a desert, crying out - only to have my words lost in the wind and blowing sand. The Cokes and Digbys have always taken great store in premonitions and the supernatural. Mama predicted the death of her first husband, Lord Andover, and Papa once heard voices at sea telling him of the location of a Spanish galleon that he later captured for The Crown. I do not know whether I can believe such stories, but Steely has made me see that my family fears for my future. They wish me to marry well, but my reckless ways may endanger that wish. Steely urges me to see finishing school as a means "to benefit from the gentler influences of the young ladies in my social class." I have promised to do my best, but I fear I shall soon tire of the polite charade.

Instead, I am determined to see my time at the Seminary for Young Ladies as an adventure - a means to learn of a strange society and people unlike me. I shall become a student of the new science of *anthropology* and study my new place and peers as an outsider - taking note of the customs of the young female English aristocrat! All the better to play the part I am asked to play, Marianne.

July 1

My farewell was an awkward one. Mama, Papa, and Steely saw me off with good wishes and promises to write soon, but I could not help but see the strange combination of relief (at my leaving?) and worry (for my prospects?) on their faces. For my part I played the dutiful daughter and charge. "Yes, I shall write too. Yes, I shall listen to my instruction. Yes, I am eager to make new friends." Yes, I shall likely drown myself in the waters of Tunbridge Wells.

I wish I could cry away my pain, but instead I find myself seething with resentment at being forced to do what I do not wish. La Madre speaks of my return at Christmas and my debut in February. I see myself galloping towards a future not of my making, but one I can see all too well. I ride towards a new home, a husband and family of my own - but will they be my own if I am not the one doing the choosing?

I do not think so, Marianne.

Tunbridge Wells
Kent, England
July 10

It has been over a week since my arrival here, and only
now do I find the time to write of my new life. The
regimen here is run with a military strictness seldom
seen at Folston, or even Holkham. Mrs. Albright, our
headmistress, runs her school much as I suspect Papa
runs his ships. Tunbridge's Rear-admiral expects
punctuality, discipline, and unquestioned respect for
the guiding principle of the seminary - the duty of
every young lady is to find a husband as socially
prominent as possible as quickly as possible. In order
to achieve this goal an entire curriculum is established:

Deportment, Custom, and Conversation
Fashion and Beauty
Voice and Singing
Piano
Art: Sketching, Watercolor, and Painting
Language: French and Italian
Dance: Cotillion, Reel, Waltz, and Quadrille
Needlework and Embroidery

Household Management

Since I received lessons from Steely, Jane, and assorted tutors in voice, piano, art, and language for years, it was deemed that only lessons in deportment, fashion, dance, embroidery, and household management were required to make me the best possible marriageable material.

I shall count down the days - all 172 of them - until Christmas when I shall return home!

Day 17

Dear Marianne, may I bore - I mean entertain - you with my typical schedule here at school?

7 a.m.
I awake to another day by a forceful knock from the maid on our chamber door. I share a room with Caroline Boyle who acts as my mentor here. In return I *fag* - run errands and complete small tasks - for her, a tradition for new students at Tunbridge. Not that I mind particularly, since Cary is unfailingly sweet, kind, and oh-so-proper. I suspect I was paired with her in the hope that those qualities would temper my rebelliousness. It has worked, so far.

As usual we sleepily complete our toilettes and help each other with our stays, making sure that they are tied loosely enough to eat a full breakfast!

8 a.m.
Back bacon. Eggs, poached, fried, or scrambled. Fried bread or toast with butter. Grilled or fried tomatoes. Sausage. Mugs of tea. Served buffet style to some thirty Anglo-Saxon girls with hearty appetites.

9 a.m.
Needlework and Embroidery. My nemeses. My chain stitch, French knots, fly stitch, back stitch, cross stitch, stem and star stitch are as skillful as a ten year old's.

10 a.m.
Household Management. According to Mrs. Albright, household management is "a skill too often left to trial and error." Too many young married ladies, in her estimation, manage their own households like their "too indulgent and often preoccupied" mothers. She clearly has not met La Madre.

11 a.m.
Deportment explained by your friend, Miss Digby:

Propriety and agreeableness are paramount to the female gender. *Custom* and *Conversation* are defined by the same. *Custom* is the code of society. *Conversation* is the communication of that code, a language in which every genteel lady must be fluent.

12-2 p.m.
Luncheon, a light repast. Unscheduled time for correspondence, reading, or napping.

3 p.m.
Fashion and Beauty. Thank God that I am blessed with good skin and hair. Really! So much bother females must go to to be attractive to the opposite sex; however, that bother must not be too obvious or the female too bold, or people may talk! As far as fashion is concerned, says common wisdom, the genteel young woman does not SET fashion, she merely FOLLOWS it. *Mon Dieu!* When I marry I shall set my own fashion and dress for my own tastes, the bolder the pattern and the brighter the colour the better.

4 p.m.
Is there any tradition more civilised than English tea time?

5-7 p.m.

Dance. I so look forward to my only exertion of my day. I enjoy the stately Cotillion and Quadrille, but the liveliness of the Reel and the romance of the Waltz cannot be matched. I wish only that I practiced them in the arms of George Anson, not the arms of Cary Boyle!

7-9 p.m.
Dinner is fashionably late. Suitable dinner conversation is practiced, at least within the hearing of our instructors.

9-10 p.m.
Preparations for bed. Candles and oil lamps extinguished by 10.

Weekends
Family visits are encouraged, as well as shopping excursions in Tunbridge. Attendance for Sunday services (Church of England, of course) is required.

Day 30

Forgive me again for not writing, Marianne. The routine here has become more mind numbing than usual by the unusual heat of late July. I am wilting in its stillness and humidity. Luckily the tedium has been broken by letters from home. Mama writes that with Papa back at

sea and my absence, she and Steely find the days hard
to fill. Luckily for us all, Mama and Steely, along with
the boys, will visit Tunbridge in a fortnight. I am so
eager to see them again!

Day 46

My family arrived yesterday and today we toured
Tunbridge. In addition to being my pleasant prison,
Tunbridge is a spa town. According to Steely, it was
made popular for tourists nearly a hundred years ago
by the dandy, Richard "Beau" Nash, who loved both
clothes and women - my governess does like her
history lessons to have a touch of scandal! However she
assures us that Beau did have strict rules concerning
behaviour when taking the waters, as well as
promoting the waters for both pleasure and health. I
suggested that we take them as well, a suggestion
seconded by Edward and Kenelm, but quickly
overruled by La Madre. She finds the sulphur smell of
the waters nauseating.

We instead walked the Pantiles where we women
admired the colonnades as the boys played on
sandstone outcrops nearby. Mama spoke of my
returning home at Christmas time and my debut at
court in March of next year with an eagerness I could

not share. The boys disappeared just as we planned to sit down to luncheon. Steely was dispatched to retrieve them and nearly an hour later returned with them in tow. With damp hair and smelling of egg from their swim in the waters, La Madre ordered the boys back to the hotel to bathe immediately and later confined them to their room with nothing to eat until supper. Odd as it might sound, I wish I could have joined them.

Day 73

Apologies again for my not writing. But as autumn approaches, the cool air has brought me a new friend, Andriana Pappas, a refuge from Greece's war of independence from the Ottoman Empire. England has opened her doors to immigrants from this nation at war. As a daughter of an important diplomat, she comes to Tunbridge to escape the turmoil and violence in her country. Small and dark with expressive hazel eyes and a low, strong voice, Andriana is my physical opposite, though our tastes are so very similar. We both play guitar, sing, love to read, and find the gossip of the other girls here too tame. She also has great skill at mimicry. Her imitation of Mrs. Albright is so skillful that she frightens unsuspecting chambermaids with surreptitious rebukes. You would like her too, Marianne!

Day 90

Andriana and I have spent our free time in the last two weeks preparing for Tunbridge's music recital. We performed Thomas Campion's *My Love Hath Vowed He Will Forsake Me,* though I feared Mrs. Albright might consider it too risque for school girls, since it speaks of a "dissembling wretch" of a man who had a young lady's "maidenhead," but she scowled only briefly at the lyrics. I must admit we sounded lovely as I accompanied Andriana's clear and true contralto with my lute. We alternated verses with her accompanying my soft soprano with guitar. Our effort was applauded generously, and we received so many compliments that I am afraid they have gone to our heads. We dream - for the moment, at least - of careers on the stage. Now wouldn't that scandalise our families and friends!

Day 100

Kenelm and Edward have finally written me as promised - in code with the Digby cipher:

Abxo Pfp,

Hbkbij xka F jfpp vlr sbov jrze, xka tb jxab mixkp ql
obpzrb vlr colj Qrkyofadb. Hbk qelrdeq qexq tb pelria
ofab lro elopbp ql Hbkq ql ebim vlr bpzxmb, yrq F qlia
efj qexq Qrkyofadb fp lsbo 100 jfibp xtxv xka qexq Jxjx
tlria yb prob ql tloov xylrq rp. F exa x ybqqbo mixk. Tb
abzfaba lk d piv zxjmxfdk. Tb pxv vlro kxjb xq ibxpq
qbk qfjbp x axv. Tb qbii pqlofbp xylrq vlr xq jbxi qfjbp.
Tb mrq vlro phbqzebp xka txqbozlilop xkvtebob Jxjx lo
Pqbbiv tfii pbb qebj. F qefkh Pqbbiv exp drbppba lro
dxjb, yrq Ix Jxaob pbbjp klq ql klqfzb. Tb tlk'q pqlm
rkqfi peb albp, xka peb ibqp vlr obqrok ql rp.

Hfppbp xka Mrkzebp,
Ba

I will translate their charming letter for you:

Dear Sis,

Kenelm and I miss you very much, and we made plans
to rescue you from Tunbridge. Ken thought that we
should ride our horses to Kent to help you escape, but I
told him that Tunbridge is over 100 miles away and
that Mama would be sure to worry about us. I had a
better plan. We decided on a sly campaign. We say your
name at least ten times a day. We tell stories about you
at meal times. We put your sketches and watercolours
anywhere Mama or Steely will see them. I think Steely

has guessed our game, but La Madre seems not to notice. We won't stop until she does, and she lets you come home to us.

Kisses and Punches.
Ed

See Marianne, it is as easy as substituting A for D!

Day 123

I have neglected you again, Marianne, but little has happened here - until today. Andriana tells me she has a lover! Like her, he is a refuge from war torn Greece. I have been sworn to secrecy regarding her clandestine meetings with him after hours. She waits until her roommate begins snoring before she slips out until early morning. I worry for her, but cannot help be thrilled by the romance of it all. She tells me that Demetri plans to return to Greece to fight for his country, and she hopes to go with him. What a dramatic turn of events! I think I am jealous.

Day 130

I returned from morning lessons today to find a letter from Andriana tucked into the latest Waverley novel I am reading. She has fled Tunbridge with Demetri early this morning. She has told me no more than the barest of details about her escape - only that they will return to Greece and marry there in the Orthodox tradition. Demetri has forbidden her to give me details, since he fears that I may betray them. I would not, of course, though I do fear the coming inquisition from Ms. Albright when Andriana is discovered missing.

Day 131

Tunbridge is abuzz with Andriana's disappearance. And as I suspected, I was brought to Ms. Albright for questioning. I told her nothing, saying that Andriana had told me little about her affair with Demetri or her plans to run away from Tunbridge. I almost feel sorry for our matron. She is clearly upset about the situation, though I suspect her worry has more to do with the school's reputation than with Andriana's safety. I must also admit to some worry, and some guilt, about not revealing the little I know, but I simply could not betray a friend's trust. She promised to write me. Until then I shall pray for their safe passage, Marianne.

Day 140

I have not heard from Andriana, though I realise it is far too early to expect a letter. I miss my friend.

Day 142

I am going home, Marianne! Mama has written to tell me the news. I am sure Edward and Kenelm will take credit for my early release, but I suspect La Madre received word of the drama here and decided that Tunbridge's supervision is too lax. Either way, I am going *home!* I leave on the first available carriage. I shall be at Forston before Advent.

Still no word of Andriana.

Forston House

Dorset, England

November 30

Sundays have always been my favourite day of the week, but never has a day been as lovely as this Advent Sunday. My homecoming has been wonderful, with only Papa's absence - who is still away at sea - keeping it from perfection. It is so good to see again the faces of those I love. Mama, Steely, Edward, Kenelm, and Jane. The servants have made Forston so beautiful with mistletoe, pine boughs, and even a yew tree decorated in the German tradition of our late Queen Charlotte. Decorated with sweets, fruits, tinsel, and wax candles, the *tannenbaum* makes our parlour so festive. I have even received an early Christmas present from Grandfather and Mama in honour of my return from Tunbridge - a sweet, young mare to replace my poor colt, Shelley. Already broken with a gentle temperament, she is unlikely to win any horse races against my brothers, but I love her nonetheless. I have named her Molly.

December 21

Papa is home for Christmas. I have not seen him for nearly six months! For the first time I have noticed the greys in his hair, not that I should be surprised. He is after all quite old, nearly fifty-four in fact. I tease him by saying that they make him look very distinguished. I told him of my friend Andriana and asked him to look into her elopement to see whether he can find any word in diplomatic channels of her whereabouts. He said he will do so, but warned me not to get my hopes up. Greece is still in turmoil.

Holkham Hall
Norfolk, England
December 25

We spend Christmas and Boxing days at Holkham,
though I am afraid our time here has become
complicated with Grandfather's marriage to Anne
Keppel and the birth of their first child, Edward.
Though only two years older than I, Anne is mistress of
a vast estate - an ownership she guards jealously from
her step-daughters, my Mama and Aunt Anne. Not only
has she taken the place of their dear mother (and the
grandmother I never knew), she has quickly produced
an heir to Holkham - all of which creates a new and
unstated awkwardness in our family relations. I
however find her fascinating. Though it is common for
girls of my social class to marry men far older than
they, the divide of fifty some years must be difficult. Yet
Anne seems genuinely fond of Grandpapa and has
clearly mastered running the domestic affairs at
Holkham. The Hall has never been more beautiful or
more efficiently run this holiday. The yuletide table was
arranged perfectly, the servants were faultless in their
service, and our Christmas goose and plum pudding

were delicious. Holkham's new Queen has even convinced her King Coke to dispense with wearing his so-very-unfashionable wig!

Perhaps such a marriage can be agreeable, Marianne.

December 27

Our tribe enjoyed Boxing Day yesterday in a tradition Grandpapa adores - the fox hunt. As his favourite granddaughter (a title I share with all my female cousins), I too adore the hunt on Boxing, though every year I secretly wish the red fox will elude us. The host of riders in their finery, the brace of the winter air, the baying of the hounds, the thrill of riding full gallop is exhilarating - almost as exhilarating as seeing cousin George Anson again.

During the hunt I rode with George's brother, Henry, my dear old friend who has been attending university at Oxford. He still insists we will marry after he returns, and I must admit that I encourage his flirtation in my poor attempts to make George jealous. Sadly he still ignores me, Marianne! Nevertheless, Henry makes a charming riding companion. We rode to Holkham's beach which, with its wide expanse at low tide, is perfect for a gallop, though my Molly is poor competition for Henry's stallion. Just before we headed back, he pulled me over for a soft kiss and a declaration that he "will always love me." I do truly wish I could return his affection.

Later we returned to the hunt where Henry witnessed his first fox kill by the hounds and received the traditional "blooding" from Grandfather. Our Master of the Hunt smeared his face with the blood of the fox. And although I have seen this gruesome tradition before, the sight of Henry's dear face covered in blood sent a peculiar chill down my spine. I thought such a sensation could only be found in novels!

1825

Forston House

Dorset, England

January 1

The new year begins with sad, sad news, Marianne. Andriana has been found dead. Papa received word from her father shortly before his departure from England for Greece. She was killed during a recent uprising in that country's civil war. Her husband, Demetri, was also killed. Poor Papa seems as shaken by the news as I. Does he imagine her death could easily have been my own?

She was four months with child.

January 15

I am to debut in March in London where I will be presented to the King. Mama, Papa, Steely and I will spend the season at our house on Harley Street.

I have no choice, Marianne.

February 2

In two days we will travel to London. I spend this Candlemas looking at my childhood home as if I will never see it again. Of course I know that I will, but I cannot help thinking that the next time I see Forston, I may well be engaged to a man I have yet to meet and will likely become a veritable guest in my old home. What an odd notion, Marianne! I find myself aimlessly walking its halls, from drawing room to library. From sitting rooms to bedrooms. From boot room to kitchen, until Cook sends me packing. So much for my exercise in nostalgia.

February 10

We leave Forston for the London season on St. Valentine's Day, an appropriate day for departure, since this season I will be hunting for a husband. Now wouldn't Mama be horrified by such coarseness! I should instead say, I will be "coming out," a peculiar but much more delicate expression, Marianne.

February 14

I am writing this after an emotional farewell this morning. The boys, who will remain at Forston with their tutors and Steely's sister, Jane, who will now act as their governess, woke early to wish all of us goodbye. As we all shared hugs, I began to weep most pathetically (I do not cry, Marianne) which caused a flood of tears from all. First, sweet Kenelm, then not-so-Steely, Mama and Jane - even dear Babou and stoic Edward brushed away a tear or two. What a sentimental lot we all are!

Harley Street
London, England
February 16

Although we have a home in London and Grandpapa is
a member of the House of Commons, we Digbys are
really country folk. We prefer open spaces and walking
or riding our horses to sitting in a sedan chair or
carriage. Papa's duties at sea also typically limit our
seasons in London since Mama is reluctant to socialise
without him. But this year we will take the city by
storm.

Let me tell you about our entrance into London
yesterday, my dear Marianne:

We ride by coach into the city through the toll gates at
Knightsbridge. From there we pass Number One, also
known as Apsley House, the residence of the Duke of
Wellington. Papa tells us that the King plans to build a
great arch nearby to commemorate the Duke's victory
over Napoleon and to mark a dramatic entry to the city.
We then pass Hyde Park to St. James Palace, the stately
home of our King, to Piccadilly Circle and onto Regent

Street. Finally we arrive at Harley Street, where the nearly identical facades of the townhouses there disguise a family crest, an azure blue shield with a *fleur-de-lis* framed by ostrich plumes that marks the doorway of 78, the residence of the Digby country mice now turned town.

February 18

We have hardly unpacked and La Madre has already planned my coming months in London. We will shop the West End in preparation for my presentation at court and for my attendance at the debutante ball. We will ride, weather permitting, at the fashionable hour of five o'clock in Hyde Park. We will meet the *haul ton*, London's social elite, at their preferred social club, Almack's. However, I am most eager to visit the British Museum with Papa as he promised me months ago. I shall see the most exotic of antiquities with the most charming of men!

February 25

Tomorrow I will finally go on my outing with dear Babou, a welcome change to the ceaseless shopping I have been doing with Mama and Steely. Who would have thought so much effort is required to merely clothe oneself? Marianne, I am poked, pinned, and prodded for hours on end! My head is measured for bonnets - and found far bigger than normal, as Steely has often claimed. My feet too are found less than desirable - a suitable length but too broad, the result of running barefoot with my brothers, says Mama. My figure however has been declared near-perfect, an attribute for which Mama claims I can thank her (though her love of chocolate has added to her girth, of late). I am fitted for all manner of dress - morning, walking, dinner, ball gown and riding habit - even an overcoat and gloves. Fashion demands it!

February 26

Papa and I rode early by carriage this cold morning to avoid the crowds at the Egyptian exhibits. Since acquiring the Rosetta Stone and other antiquities from Napoleon, Montague House, home to our British Museum, has burst at the seams with its mighty collections - so much so that a new and much larger Greco-Roman building is now being planned to house them all, according to Papa. I though cannot imagine a more intriguing display of archaeological finds than what I saw today. First we saw the Rosetta Stone. This large, though unimposing black stone includes text in three languages: Ancient Greek, Ancient Egyptian script and hieroglyphics. Now scholars, due to the recent efforts of Champollion, can decipher the strange symbols inscribed on the many wonderful frescos in the collection. Next we saw a royal sarcophagus thought to be Alexander the Great's which was rescued from its ignoble use as a bathtub in Alexandra, as well as gigantic granite statues of royalty whose names I can neither remember nor pronounce. But the most haunting "artifact" we saw was a mummy. The stained linen-wrapped body was prepared to preserve it for the soul's afterlife. As I stared at the remains, I had an odd and disturbing thought. I wondered whether a lost Egyptian soul could find its body in England. It seems such a long way to travel.

March 1

I am to be presented at the court of King George IV in a fortnight. Mama worries whether my white silk gown and gloves will be completed by the seamstress in time, and whether white ostrich feathers for my hair might be excessive. She worries that I will forget a proper curtesy or forms of address. She tells me that she worries that I do not worry enough. After all, my entire future is at stake. I must make a good impression. What if I am saucy with the King? Papa, Steely, and I assure her that I will not embarrass her, that I have been raised well - well enough to know that I should not say what I think. I have you for that, dear Marianne!

March 16

It is now official. Today Lady Andover (Mama, of course) presented me to King George IV. Also in attendance was Lady Conyngham (the King's mistress), Lady Jersey (his former mistress), Countess of Oxford (who is said to have had a torrid affair with Lord Byron despite being twice his age), and Princess Esterhazy (an infamous patroness of Almack's Assembly Rooms).

Mama told me that I made such a good impression that the Princess will recommend approval for vouchers to Almack's. Mama expects that I shall make "imminent conquests." I thought the King very fat.

March 18

The weather has finally turned spring, and I shall go riding in Hyde Park. Not alone, of course. My every move is shadowed. I am now an adult in principle, if not in practice. I may not walk alone, ride alone, or shop alone. I must consider my reputation. An appropriate chaperone - father, mother, governess, trusted family friend or groom - is required at all times or people will talk. And that kind of talk may destroy an unmarried young lady's marriage prospects. All this fuss to preserve her virtue, or at least the appearance or it, Marianne!

Today I am accompanied by Mama as we ride in our barouche carriage, which is driven by a coachman and is open to the fair weather. Our destination is Rotten Row, or *Route du Roi*, where the fashionable are seen by those fashionable. As absurd as my situation is, it *is* heavenly to feel the warm sun on my face, to hear the rhythmic clap of horse hooves, to smell the early bulbs in bloom, and to see beautiful La Madre smiling. Lady Andover in her element. We exchange pleasantries with all we meet since, according to Mama, only the best people can ride The King's Row - no hired hacks allowed! For me, I must become accustomed to the appraising looks I get from those we meet. Mothers and fathers with marriageable sons see me as a potential daughter-in-law; mothers and fathers with marriageable daughters see me as competition. I find myself uncharacteristically shy. But no matter, I am here to be seen, not heard.

March 20

Last night I danced until two at the debutante ball. What a peculiar sensation to feel the touch of a man to whom you are not related in dancing a cotillion or quadrille! Before I had only danced with Papa, Grandpapa, Edward, Kenelm, or the girls at finishing school. But to be so close to a young man, to hold one hand and to feel the other upon your back - how lovely. It is unfortunate that the waltz was deemed too risque for debutantes. How *so* provincial.

Though as much as I enjoyed dancing, the conversation at the buffet was awkward. The debutantes tittered and giggled in their white silk gowns. The same young men in tailcoats whose touch I enjoyed on the dance floor were as tongue-tied as I at the table, some even had the unfortunate habit of staring at my decolletage! Still, tomboy I may be, I am feminine enough to enjoy the power of being found attractive. Now, if I could only learn to flirt, Marianne.

March 22

This Wednesday night Mama and Papa are taking me to Almack's. Our approved vouchers have been purchased for ten guineas each. The Digbys are now part of the London elite - if not *haul ton*, at least a half ton! Really

Marianne, the fashionable patronesses of Almack's take their social etiquette so very, very seriously. Papa says that the Duke of Wellington was once denied entry to Almack's for wearing long trousers. Mama says Lady Caroline Lamb, after having written about one scandalous patroness of Almack's in one of her novels, was barred from the club in retaliation. We really must all be on our best behavior or be brought low by high society.

March 25

Princess Esterhazy and Countess Lieven, the lovely Patronesses of Almack's, made us very welcomed last night. And with their evident approval I was made much fuss over by the young men in attendance. I was even given a nickname, *Light of Day*, to which I responded, "Don't be absurd!" Though secretly the name pleased me, so much so that I could imagine Steely warning me of the dangers of taking flattery too seriously. I chose to ignore her! I even learned the art of flirtation with the Princess and Countess as my teachers. I carefully studied how they raised their chins as they laughed, smiled as they flipped open their fans, and rolled their eyes as they issued clever epigrams. Oh Marianne, to be a woman of the world!

April 4

I met someone. Edward Law, Lord Ellenborough. We
met at Almack's on my eighteenth birthday. Early in the
evening he introduced himself to Mama and Papa and
reminded them that they had met once before at
Holkham, when he had visited Grandfather regarding
their work in Parliament. He then asked me to dance, a
waltz, with their approval of course. They approved. I
accepted. Fortunately, Almack's has no prohibition
against the waltz, a dance thought by some to lead to
"licentious consequences." No such consequences
occurred with Lord Ellenborough, though I must admit
the waltz is more intimate than a quadrille or cotillion -
and private conversation with one's partner so much
easier, though I spoke little. Edward, as he demanded I
call him, told me that my silence reminded him of
Aurora Raby in Byron's poem, *Don Juan*. I asked him
whether that would make him the legendary Don Juan,
to which he laughed and asked me, "Do you think me as
old as that?" Luckily the dance ended before I had time
to answer, and he returned me to my parents with a
deep bow.

He really is very handsome with his tousled brown
curls. A fact of which he seems not unaware.

April 5

Mama has made inquiries into the background of Lord
Ellenborough. He is thirty-five, a wealthy widower
without children. His peerage is recent, though his
political connections in the House of Lords are wide
and his ambitions great, according to her sources. Not
surprisingly, he met with her approval. She did not ask
me whether he met with mine.

April 6

Lord Ellenborough has asked Papa's permission to
court me. Papa has agreed. Edward and I will ride by
carriage to Regent's Park this Saturday afternoon with
Steely as chaperone.

April 8

Why am I so nervous, Marianne? When I am nervous I
grow silent, and I grow more silent with each passing
day. Steely has noticed and has declared the loss of my
chatterbox ways a "marked improvement." She tells me
that men love a good listener. I wonder how she might
know this, since she is a spinster. An uncharitable

thought, I know, Marianne. But I hardly think Edward wants a mute wife!

April 11

I have just returned from my outing with Edward. He arrived looking dashing in his *Phaeton*. I sat beside him as he drove, while Steely sat in the rear seat, out of our sight but within earshot. We talked of the fine spring weather and the flowering cherry trees. We then spoke to the fineness of Grandpapa's arboretum at Holkham. We moved from tree to horseflesh as I remarked on the beauty of his Friesians. He allowed me to take the reins and complimented me on my strong hand with them. Then Steely, no doubt overwhelmed by such scintillating conversation, called out from her seat behind us and told Edward of my fearless riding skills. He responded by asking me whether I would like to go riding someday, to which I responded, "Certainly." And so it regrettably went . . . until we returned home to Harley Street.

Oh dear Marianne, what can an eighteen-year-old girl really have to say to a man almost twice her age, and he to her?

April 13

A letter from Edward has arrived by post earlier today.
He apologised for the awkwardness of our meeting on
Saturday and confessed to a discomfort, since his wife's
death, with small talk - a discomfort which keeps him
from easy sociability. He also enclosed, to my great
surprise and pleasure, a lovely poem addressed to me -

Fair Janet,
I beg you.
Do not be impatient with my rustic ways.
Past love now gone
Has caused me such pain
That I thought never to hope to love again,
Until I saw you,
A young and sweet rose.
I dare now to hope.

Oh Marianne, I dare to hope as well.

April 14

I have spent most of last evening working on my reply
to Edward's letter. Though I fear I am far more

proficient with prose than verse, I completed this short
poem in time for the morning post:

You say you dare to hope.
I too dare to dream upon a future -
Where this Janet might find my own
Waiting tomorrow night,
Unmasked yet not undone.

Am I too bold, Marianne?

April 15

Fair Janet and her own Edward raised more than a few
eyebrows at Almack's tonight. We refused to dance
with anyone else, though social rules clearly indicate
that a young lady should never dance more than once
with any one partner. Luckily for us, Princess Esterhazy
proclaimed that some rules are made to be broken. A
proclamation seconded by Countess Lieven. Lady
Andover sighed with relief.

May 25

Pardon, Pardon, Pardon, my Marianne. I have neglected
you for over five weeks. I have no excuse. Except love.

Edward has proposed marriage! He will ask Papa's permission for my hand tonight.

May 26

Papa has agreed, as I knew he would! He likes and respects Edward. Mama and Steely are also so very pleased. And even though we are all breathless from the swift courtship, Edward will ask the Archbishop to waive a required publishing of the marriage banns so that we may wed as soon as possible. My oh-so-eager fiance!

May 30

La Madre has turned her organizational zeal to a new ambitious project - a marriage in less than four months! The first order of business is my trousseau. Next, it has been decided that we will visit Edward's family and his estates at Roehampton and in Connaught Place (I shall be a city girl now, Marianne!) Then we all must visit Forston and Holkham to introduce *my* Lord Ellenborough to the Digby-Coke-Anson clan. Finally, the marriage ceremony must be planned. I count the days!

June 5

Today, Mama and Steely took me to my last fitting for my trousseau. Undergarments - petticoats, chemises, corsets - were the bridal clothes sought today. I was also fitted for what the shop girl assured us is the latest in French fashion, the *negligee*, whose sheerness made Steely blush! Attire for the bedroom, but not for sleep, I mused.

June 7

Now that I am officially engaged much of my freedom has been restored to me. Evidently engagement bestows a trust not found by those *sans* betrothal. I now may ride with Edward *alone*. We now may kiss without Steely, my English *duenna*, looking on. And although I have little basis for comparison, Edward's thorough kisses fill me with such hunger and longing. When he holds me in his arms and murmurs, *my Janet*, I come undone.

I feel his sweet touch even in my dreams.

June 12

Mama, Papa, and I spent the day at Edward's country home just outside of London, where we met my prospective in-laws - Elizabeth, his sister and Charles, his brother. Also in attendance, strangely enough, were the Londonderrys, the parents of Edward's wife, Octavia, who died five years ago. They all made much fuss over me, though Elizabeth especially so, saying that she had always wanted a younger sister and hoped we would become fast friends. I do, as well. The Londonderrys, on the other hand, regaled Mama and Papa with Edward's many virtues as a son-in-law and congratulated me on my fine match, a breach of etiquette not lost on La Madre! Luckily Edward and I soon escaped our families with a private tour of Elm Grove, his lovely home - a home we will soon share.

When he gathers me in his arms, I too believe no match could be finer.

June 30

Edward and I spent the last day of the season at a flight of a hot air balloon in Westminster by the famed aeronaut, Charles Green. As we watched his ascent, I imagined that we too could fly over rooftops of London, soar over its countryside, and ride the winds to destinations unfamiliar and untouched. Instead Edward must return to his work in Parliament, while I return home, waiting impatiently until late July when he visits Forston and Holkham to meet my family. How shall I endure the hours, Marianne?

Forston House

Dorset, England

July 3

Although I am already missing Edward, it is good to be home. We arrived long after dark last night and quietly made our way to bed without waking the household. It was not until morning that I was rudely woken by my brothers who burst into my room followed by an apologetic Jane. They asked all kinds of ill-mannered questions about Edward. "Is he really as old as Grandpapa?" "Is he as rich?" "Can we come visit you in London after you marry?" To which I answered, "No," "No," and "Yes, if you let me sleep a little longer." Just then Papa bellowed from across the hall, "Boys, leave your sister be!" The command from the Rear-admiral sent them packing, while Jane whispered, "We'll talk later," and softly closed the door. I slept long past nine o'clock, dreaming of him.

July 11

I spend my days in old girlish pursuits. I ride Molly for hours. I fight with my brothers for nearly as long. I sketch and watercolour landscapes of Folston, trying to capture the brick of her facade and the green of her hills. I pick guitar and lute listlessly. I gossip about the denizens of Almack's with Jane. I complain to Steely about no word from Edward. She makes the matter worse by telling me that he is a busy man who has more important things to do than write letters to spoiled young ladies. My complaints however make enough impression upon her that she has Mama speak to me about the responsibilities of being a wife to an ambitious man. I am ashamed enough to keep silent my frustrations.

July 12

He writes, Marianne! He tells me what I must hear. *In verse.* He misses me as I miss him, though he takes comfort in the knowledge that soon "heaven will be realised on earth" and that he will find "love's ecstasy in my arms".

Has a girl ever been courted more ardently?

July 25

Yesterday Edward arrived at Forston for the week to meet with my family and to see Forston House. He came bearing gifts: a paper theatre for the boys, Cuban cigars for Papa, flowers and candy for Mama, Steely, and Jane. How wonderful to see his handsome face and to hear his deep voice again. I am so very proud of him. I was also proud to show off my family home - from its parapets to urns, from its oak staircase to its terraced alcoves, from its green lawns to its flower gardens. He was so impressed by the tour that he rewarded his guide with a lingering kiss. I cannot wait to show him the house and grounds of Holkham this weekend!

I have found during our visit to Holkham that some political tensions lie between Grandpapa and Edward. You see, Edward supported King George's unsuccessful bid to divorce Queen Caroline, while Grandpapa very much did not. And while Tom Coke is a member of the House of Commons, my intended is a member of the House of Lords.

I do not care much for politics. I cannot understand why men must see the issues of the day in such extremes. They stand for and against as Whig or Tory - see the world in black and white. Instead I see colour - red, green, and blue - and shades between, blended to create a world single and separate from party and principles. However, I am certain both Edward and Grandpapa would see such ideas as foolish and romantic, Marianne.

In spite of these tensions, our visit was a success. As I did at Forston, I acted as Edward's tour guide, only this time on horseback. Will, our groom from Forston, helped us choose mounts from Holkham's fine stables. We rode through the miles of lawn, through the greenhouse and gardens and stopped to picnic at the lake I swam naked in just two summers ago. How I have matured since then!

Edward charmed my Coke and Anson relatives, especially my Aunt Anne and my young step-grandmother, Anne. He flirted most charmingly with them both, so much so that I wished my cousins George and Henry were here so that I might do the same! But I shall not worry about Edward's reputation with women. I know in my heart that his belongs to me.

Harley Street

London, England

August 11

Mama, Papa, Steely and I have returned to London to make final preparations for the wedding and to attend important social engagements. Edward and I are to dine with the Duke of Wellington at his London home. Oh Marianne, I do hope I make a good impression.

August 15

Tonight we dined with the Duke at Apsley House. I managed to conquer my nerves with Edward at my side, though the man who defeated Napoleon at Waterloo is formidable. His countenance is handsome and stern, his voice a deep baritone with a soft suggestion of Irish lilt. His wife, Kitty, on the other hand, is as soft and plump as the Duke is hard and lean. She squinted and giggled nervously throughout dinner, but kindly spoke to me of my upcoming marriage and congratulated Edward on winning "such a sweet girl."

Yet I saw no tenderness between her and the Duke and suspect their marriage is an unhappy one.

Edward later told me that the Duke may well become Prime Minister and that my conduct at dinner made him proud. His words reassure me that despite my youth I will be a fitting partner to my husband's ambitions.

September 1

In two weeks we will be married. *Final* plans have *finally* been made for our wedding day, September 15 - just over six months since we first met. We will have the ceremony at 78 Harley Street.

Just yesterday Mama, Steely, and I together visited Edward's townhome at Connaught Place near Hyde Park. Edward will be close neighbours to his in-laws, Marianne! During our visit my husband-to-be asked that we make suggestions for my living there, so that he could have improvements made during our honeymoon at Brighton. How very thoughtful he is!

September 14

Tomorrow I will become Lady Ellenborough. Mama and I have finally chosen which gown from my trousseau I will wear for the ceremony - a beautiful one of soft blue, green and amber which suits my pink and gold colouring. We will marry early in the morning in my parent's drawing room with Edward's uncle, Bishop of Bath and Wells, performing the ceremony with only close family and friends in attendance. After a buffet luncheon, we leave for the Norfolk Arms at Brighton for three weeks.

You would think I would be nervous, but instead it is Mama who is on edge. She rushes about frantically, arranging the recently delivered wedding flowers, barking orders to the chambermaids about overlooked cobwebs, and absentmindedly stroking my hair every time she walks by me. I remain curiously calm. Am I so confident in my choice of Edward? Yes.

Everyone has been so sweet to me of late. The boys, who arrived with Jane just two nights ago, entertained Mama, Papa, Edward and me with a charming (and slightly indelicate) play about our courtship and impending marriage with their toy theatre. Jane has given me a lovely sketch and watercolour of Forston, putting my own poor efforts to shame. My dear Steely has embroidered me a pretty handkerchief of blue roses, so that I might carry something both blue and new before the Bishop. Mama has loaned me her mother's antique pearl strands so that she and her maid, Cecilia, might dress my hair with them for the wedding. Papa has contributed a *very* generous dowry as part of my marriage contract. And last but never least I received by post just moments ago a sonnet addressed to his *Ianthe* - Greek for Jane - from my Lord, Edward.

Sussex, England

September 23

Nights are indeed made for loving.

I never imagined a wedding bed could offer such pleasure. I, of course, as any country girl might, understood how the act was accomplished. And I knew from rather frank discussion among the girls at Tunbridge that some women enjoyed the act. I even knew what was expected of me - bear and forbear mostly - from Madame Lanfear's marriage manual thrust upon me by a blushing Steely. But Marianne, I never thought such delight could be found in the arms of a patient lover! And more - well, possibly more - wonderful than the act itself was the tenderness expressed by Edward during and after - just thinking about it makes me sigh. Really, such intimacy is wholly, utterly, and perfectly satisfactory.

September 25

The King, when Prince Regent, made Brighton a fashionable retreat for the fashionable set. According to Edward, the Prince had his Royal Pavilion built here as a discreet rendezvous for his mistress, Maria Fitzherbert, when he was denied a divorce from the Queen. However there is nothing discreet about its architecture which was created by the great John Nash. The blend of Indian and Muslim design with its white domes and minarets reminds me of paintings I have seen of the Taj Mahal. Both palaces too were created in the name of love. How fittingly romantic for a honeymoon!

The brace of the salt air and the warmth of the autumn sun on the beach at Brighton also lends itself to long walks along the sea, marred only by the occasional sand pebble found in a shoe. My bonnet and parasol have protected me from the sun, though Edward has become quite brown. It suits him, and I now call him my gypsy lover and admire the contrast of his dark fingers intertwined with my white. On one I wear a gold posy ring formed with delicate filigree that is inscribed with a hidden message from Edward, "My heart is thine." Time moves so slowly here that I see each moment clearly. As Miss Austen writes:

Nobody could catch cold by the sea; nobody wanted appetite by the sea; nobody wanted spirits; nobody wanted strength. Sea air was healing, softening, relaxing - fortifying and bracing - seemingly just as was wanted - sometimes one, sometimes the other. If the sea breeze failed, the sea bath was the certain corrective; and where bathing disagreed, the sea air alone was evidently designed by nature for the cure.

Though I suspect Miss A was being a tad ironic in her descriptions of the powers of the seaside, I believe them to be true.

September 26

Oh Marianne, Edward and I just had our first disagreement. I shall not call it a quarrel, since no voices were raised or unkind words said. He wished to spend the afternoon bathing in the sea. Well and good for him, I thought, since he could swim naked on the gentlemen's beach. I however must not only bathe on the beach for ladies, but must also be wheeled out upon the water in a ridiculous contraption called a bathing machine, wearing an equally ridiculous bathing gown in which weights are placed to prevent it from floating upward and revealing more than a proper lady should. When I suggested that we instead swim naked later under the cover of night, he replied that as tempting as that sounded we must protect our reputations. I answered without thinking, "You mean *your* reputation?" He responded by giving me a sharp look and a quick bow and left without a word. I sit here anxiously awaiting his return.

September 27

Edward returned hours later, hair damp and smelling of the ocean. I begged him to forgive my sharp words. He replied by gathering me into his arms and carrying me to our bed. He tasted of salt.

October 3

We are on our last days at Brighton. I hate the idea of our time here coming to a close and my having to share Edward with London. I asked him how I would spend my days without my family. "Why, we may have already started our own, darling," he replied. A child. Of course. How curious that the idea leaves me cool.

Connaught Place
London, England
October 8

We arrived in London yesterday, and Edward has already returned to his duties in Parliament. I do so want to be a good wife to him, but I am afraid my experience with domestic management is limited to the instruction given at Tunbridge Wells and observing Mama. Organization has never been a strength of mine, and I am already at sixes and sevens with how to deal with the servants and how to find a good lady's maid. How fortunate that La Madre has written a primer for Coke chatelaines. I will read it at once.

October 9

Oh Marianne, Mama's advice is so very . . . disagreeable. In her primer, she speaks of what servants must or must not be and what they must and must not do. For instance, a lady's maid "must *not* have a will of her own in *anything*, and always be good-humoured and approve of everything her mistress likes" and she "must *run* the instant she is called whatever she is about. Morning, noon and night she must not mind going without sleep." And so it goes. Poor Cecilia to have such demands upon her, if indeed Mama demands such behaviour of her *own* maid! I shall *not* be so demanding. I hope to find a companion, perhaps even a friend, in my own choice.

I discovered this morning that our honeymoon did not produce a child.

October 15

After many interviews and recommendations, I have finally found my personal maid. Upon hearing her sad story, I hired Eugenie immediately. You see, Marianne, after a love affair with a married man ended with her with child, Eugenie's family forced her to give up the child, a daughter, to be fostered by the man and his wife. *Quelle horreur!* She is only a year older than I, French, petite and very pretty. She and I have decided to improve our English and French respectively by speaking only in the other's native tongue when alone. *Ce que c'est drôle!*

October 17

Edward has given me the most beautiful sapphire and emerald pendant necklace as a reward for my patience with his spending so many hours with work after our return from Brighton. Eugenie tells me it is good for a husband to feel guilty about spending too much time away from his new wife. I agree, of course! I will wear the necklace when Edward and I attend Almack's tonight.

October 18

Edward and I spoke with my cousin, George Anson, last night at Almack's. He offered his belated congratulations and well wishes on our marriage. He also told us that he is soon to resign his army commission as colonel to serve as a member of Parliament. George is still quite dashing, but he cannot hold a candle to my darling husband who was so sweet and attentive that I could hardly wait to return home. *Comment je suis méchant, Marianne!*

November 1

I hosted a ladies luncheon, a small one with La Madre, Steely, who now acts as Mama's companion, Auntie Anson, and Edward's sister, Elizabeth. Despite my nervousness, my first attempt at entertaining went swimmingly. Mama approves of my choice of Eugenie, saying that "the French always make the best maids." Of course, I failed to mention Eugenie's *romantic* past! Elizabeth tells me that she is "delighted to see her brother looking so happy." I complain to the ladies about Edward's long hours at work and my learning to fill the days without him, to which my aunt remarks that she hopes my days may soon be filled with "new obligations," to which I respond, "Edward and I are trying our best." All laugh, with the exception of a *too* easily shocked Steely.

November 9

I am not with child. I find the waiting most difficult, Marianne.

November 10

How *do* I fill my days, Marianne? What follows is a sketch of a typical day in the life of your Lady Ellenborough:

I awake to the sound of Edward speaking softly to his manservant, Henry, in his adjoining bedroom. I ring for

Eugenie to help with my morning toilette, so that I might have a light breakfast and tea with him before he leaves for Parliament. We speak of coming social engagements and needed household repairs, as I read *La Belle Assemblee* and *The Morning Post*. Edward then leaves at 10 o'clock for his office in Westminster. I spend much of the morning speaking to Cook about the week's menu and to our formidable housekeeper, Mrs. Danvers - cribbing from my innumerable to-do lists about daily chores and shopping planned. I then sit down to neglected household accounts and correspondence until a luncheon of cold meats, bread, cheese, and fruit with tea.

During the afternoon hours I make my social calls, typically friends from Almack's, Edward's sister, and of course Mama and Papa when they are in London. Sometimes we go shopping together or visit the art galleries on Pall Mall. When I return, and if weather permits, I ride Molly in Hyde or Regent's Park. I then return home to wait for Edward. I nap, read, write in my not-so-weekly diary (apologies, my dear), sketch or practise my music. By 7 o'clock we typically sit down to dinner. After dessert we play cards, whisk if we have company, attend the theatre, or dance at Almack's until 11 or 12. When we return home, we retire to our respective bedchambers - or not - until another day begins.

November 17

Edward and I will hold our first dinner party in little more than a fortnight. Mama arrived earlier today to help me write cards for those invited and to offer her motherly advice. What follows are the steps required for the preparation and the execution of the perfect dinner party by Lady Andover, as interpreted by your Lady Ellenborough:

1. One must take care to invite the proper quantity and quality of dining companions. For our party the number deemed most conducive to lively and sociable conversation is twelve with, of course, an equal number of ladies and gentlemen. Great care must also be taken with the age and disposition of those invited, according to La Madre. A party dominated by the young may result in witty and spirited repartee, but the calming influence of the mature will temper those spirits. Thus, a mix of young and old is required. As for the dispositions of those concerned, a mix is also suggested - those who listen well and ask interesting questions and those who are talkative and never leave a question, interesting or not, unanswered.

2. Now, the seating of both diners and table must be considered, as well as a bill of fare carefully planned. Custom recommends alternating male and female guests, but husbands and wives should *never* be placed side-by-side. Really, what could they possibly have to say to one another? In addition, the table must be arranged in such a way that the butler and footman can easily serve guests food and beverage with minimal intrusion. Soup is to be served first, followed by an entree of breads and vegetables with sauces. The main course of fish, fowl, or meat is then served, followed by a cheese course to aid in digestion, and ending with dessert. Of course, a variety of wines are provided with each course, along with fermented drink, though the latter may have the unfortunate tendency to produce gas.

3. Finally, it is the duty of the hostess to make sure that the Cook and kitchen staff keep pace with each course completed and to make sure all courses arrive upon the table the appropriate temperature. In addition, both hostess and host should keep dinner conversation well-paced and appropriate, making sure that a lull is filled with entertaining questions, or that a topic ill-advised is steered to more suitable ones. After dinner the

men will remain in the dining room for coffee, port or brandy, and pipes or cigars, while the ladies retire to the drawing room for tea, coffee, or hot chocolate until such time as ennui or fatigue shall mercifully claim them.

Pray for me, Marianne!

December 4

Last night's dinner went far better than I anticipated, though far from the perfection hoped for by Mama. The white soup was rather cool; the veal rather overcooked, she deemed. I now have the unenviable task of speaking to Cook about her shortcomings! The Duke of Wellington's wife, Kitty, was also unable to attend, pleading a sick headache at the last moment, making for a very awkward breach in the sitting arrangements, according to La Madre. Who knew an empty chair could be so vexing? Our company however met with much approval, especially the members of the King's Cottage Clique: the Duke, the Prince and Princess Esterhazy, and the Count and Countess Lieven. With the help of my dear sister-in-law, I had prepared a list of questions earlier - should there be any lull in the conversation at the table - but Elizabeth, Mama, and the gregarious Princess and Countess made sure no such lull occurred.

I am certain the gentlemen - Papa, the Counts, the Duke, Edward, and Elizabeth's husband - were eager to retreat to the library for their cigars and brandy.

I sometimes feel I am acting a part for which I am ill-suited.

December 8

Four months have passed, and I am still not with child. Edward spends such hours in work that I am not surprised.

Elm Grove
Roehampton, England
December 20

We have left the city for the holiday season. I must admit to feeling much more at home at Roehampton than Connaught Place. I am a country girl at heart, much more comfortable upon horseback than trading witty puns and barbs with the *haul ton*. Here Edward is not distracted by debates and politics. In fact, he is as ardent as a newly married groom - and I am his very satisfied bride! Just yesterday he slipped a poem under my pillow before his morning ride. In one stanza he pleads,

"Love me as you have done,
And I will love you ever so."

To which I reply,

"I ask no more
As you are now,
To her whose fate in him is bound."

We are foolish romantics, are we not?

December 25

To think just last year at this time I despaired of my future. But now I can imagine a brilliant future with Edward. This Christmas day has bestowed such gifts upon us. To Edward I have given a gold pen and a miniature of me in my wedding gown and sapphire and emerald pendant, painted by William Charles Ross. He loves both pen and painting, but confessed his surprise that I was able to sit still long enough to have my portrait done! In return he gave me a green box of stunning jewels, heirlooms from his family, which he suggests I have remounted to suit my tastes. We also gave the servants both here and at Connaught holiday pay and leave, as Edward and I depart for Forston and family tomorrow.

But for now we enjoy the cool winter weather with a long ride together, followed by a dinner of Christmas goose and a warm fire. I sing *Silent Night* and *I Saw Three Ships in Morning* as I play guitar and lute. Edward reads aloud in his husky baritone the Christmas story from Luke, Chapter Two. I paint a portrait of domestic bliss, do I not, Marianne?

1826

Elm Grove

Roehampton, England

January 3

Edward and I have returned from the holidays at
Forston to Roehampton for a few days until we leave
for London for his return to Parliament. Our Christmas
visit was lovely, of course, though I must admit that I
did not see enough of Papa, my brothers, or Edward, for
that matter. I am beginning to realise that my married
status requires me to spend much of my time with
other women! I did however enjoy seeing Steely and
Jane again and visiting Holkham for the Boxing Day fox
hunt. The holiday season has passed far too quickly, but
I should trust in what the coming months will hold.

The truth, Marianne? I dread the winter to come. The London season begins in March, and until then I suspect only debate and politics will occupy my Edward.

Connaught Place
London, England
January 10

I believe I may be with child. I cannot be certain, but I am late, and I am never late.

January 11

I have told Eugenie of my hope, and of my fears. I turn to her as I turn to you, Marianne, as a sympathetic friend. She offers gentle advice with only my best interests at heart. She suggests that I wait another month, so that I am sure, before I tell Edward.

More waiting.

January 18

I toss and turn, from anxiety to delight and back again. I am terrible at keeping secrets, but Edward does not appear to notice my agitated state. I am almost glad, since I am even worse at deception than I am at secret keeping.

January 29

I am unwell, and I am rarely unwell. For the past few days I have had piercing headaches. I am nauseous all morning and afternoon, but by supper I am ravenous. I sleep like the dead, but I am always tired. Eugenie agrees with me that I am certainly with child and that Edward should be told the happy news.

January 30

Edward is so happy that my own worry and concern have vanished. He insists that I sleep late, plies me with sweets, and forbids me to ride. He spoils me with a triple strand of freshwater pearls. I am indeed a spoiled lady of leisure, Marianne. Now, if I could only keep down breakfast!

I must write Mama.

February 7

Mama and Steely have arrived from Folston for the week. Although La Madre claims she is far too young to be a grandmother, I can see how happy she is at my news. She has given me a coral necklace as a talisman for her first grandchild. She tells me that she will write to Papa, who is again at sea, about "the blessed event." Steely too is proud of me. She says she will begin sewing cotton frocks for "the little one." To think that the most natural of functions can bring such joy and approval.

February 10

I just received a lovely note from Papa:

My Dear Janie -

Your mother has managed to get word to me in Calais before we set sail for Gibraltar. Words cannot express how pleased I am with the news. I cannot believe that my sweet girl will soon be a mother. The years have passed far too swiftly for me. Be brave and trust in those who love you. I will see you come spring, Till then, my dear.

- Your darling Babou

February 13

I am so frightened, Marianne. I woke this morning with the most terrible bleeding. Eugenie has gone to fetch Mama.

March 10

I lost our child.

I have spent much of the past month in the haze of opium tincture, prescribed by a London chemist for any womanly troubles. With each bitter sip I suffered no pain from my loss, only a sluggish euphoria of mind and body - until the last drop was gone. Now persistent agitation claims me. I cannot sleep. My muscles ache. My nose and eyes water most dreadfully. Those I love look over me with a curious mix of tenderness and worry.

March 23

Each day of late I reclaim more and more of myself. The days now begin earlier with spring approaching, and I greet them happily. Mama and Steely no longer shadow my every step. Papa and the boys have written to tell me of their joy at my recovery. Edward smiles again.

April 3

My nineteenth birthday! Today I was judged well enough to go carriage riding in Hyde Park. We rode in Edward's phaeton, the same one we rode on our awkward first outing some months ago. He gave me a butterfly brooch with emerald eyes that he expects me to wear when we attend Almack's next Wednesday. The London season has begun without us, Marianne!

April 7

I do not believe that I have *properly* introduced Almack's Assembly Rooms:

Located on King Street, St James, Almack's is the *most* exclusive social club in London, and the only one in which both men and women may attend. Every Wednesday evening from March to June during *the* season, London's elite come to see and be seen. Almack's consists of a huge ballroom lighted with cut glass chandeliers and decorated with mirrors and gilded columns in the fashionable Grecian-Roman style.

A balcony for the small orchestra lies at one end of the ballroom, while a raised dais lies at the other. Here the Lady Patronesses hold court. Refreshments are limited - lemonade or weak tea (no strong drink permitted!) and biscuits or bread and butter. But no matter, all come to dance, to gossip, to find scandal - or all three - in abundance.

Tonight Edward and I are admitted into the Assembly Rooms, but only after the doorman is given a slight nod from Princess Esterhazy. We evidently fulfill Almack's most exacting standards. From there we greet and are greeted by some of the establishment's most illustrious and most notorious members: the Duke of Wellington and his current mistress, Harriet Arbuthnot, and her *very understanding* husband Charles, Lady Sarah Jersey, another Patroness, who despite her nickname *Silence*, can never stop talking, and the witty Thomas Creevey, a diarist who we fear records our every conversation.

After our welcome, we head to the dance floor. Here we meet the plump George Cruikshank, the celebrity *du jour* who skewers politicians and the *haul ton* with sly caricatures, dancing with the slender Countess de Lieven. While Edward and I waltz, I spy -

Viscount Petersham leaning precariously as he sips not-so-discreetly from a silver flask (and I thought he was strictly a tea drinker!), Lord and Lady Londonderry, having an argument - I mean a spirited discussion - at the refreshment buffet, and poetess Caroline Lamb with high colour and in a state of dishabille leaving the backroom in the company of an attractive young man.

With such *le petit* dramas to entertain us, we pass our Wednesday night until Thursday morning, when our coach comes to collect us. Edward is oh-so-affectionate on the ride home, so much so that we eagerly make our way to his bedchamber upon our arrival home. Oh Marianne, it is lovely to be well again!

April 17

Mama and Steely returned home nearly ten days ago, leaving me very alone. Since our wonderful night at Almack's, I have seen Edward less than an hour or two a day. He leaves before I awake and though he arrives promptly for dinner, he retreats to his bed chambers shortly after. I have asked if anything is wrong, and he tells me that he must spend more hours at work since he lost so much time at home during my illness. "Of course," I reply.

I am not with child.

May 1

Matching amethyst bracelets awaited me at breakfast, a gift from Edward. I would have preferred a long walk together in Regency Park this beautiful May Day.

May 8

I believe I am compared to a memory, and found wanting. I have been told that Octavia, Edward's first wife, was a paragon: beautiful, accomplished, and kind. It is she that stands between Edward and me. He loves her still.

I am jealous of a ghost, Marianne.

May 16

Edward complains that I am "no longer gay." I compose a poem to him telling him of my fears concerning Octavia and ask, "Did her passion equal mine?" He responds with a short note left for me on my bed stand, telling me that I am "foolish for thinking Octavia stands between us" and assures me that "all is well."

All is not.

May 20

I never thought I could be so angry.

With an anger so hot I paced the floor again and again. I would have wept if I could. I would have screamed if I thought no one would hear me.

I discovered a sketch in Edward's bedchamber. Of a woman, rather young and rather pretty. On the reverse, written in an unsteady hand the words, *For my darling Edward. From your love, Maggie.*

I wait for darling Edward's return.

May 21

Edward denies all. He says the sketch was given to him by a confectioner's daughter who fancies herself in love with him - a love he does not return. He offers me a convenient lie. I shall not take it.

I leave for home tomorrow.

May 22

I write to you Marianne as I ride by coach to Forston. I stole away after breakfast with Eugenie in tow. Edward does not know. I simply told Mrs. Danvers that I am visiting my parents in Dorset. He may make of that what he will.

I was a romantic fool to think he pined for his late wife, when he had other diversions. A confectioner's daughter. How very cheap of him.

Forston House

Dorset, England

May 23

I am home. I have told Steely and Mama that I fled
London to escape the heat and smell of the city in late
spring, that I had become bored with Edward's
unrelenting schedule in Parliament which leaves little
time for me. Steely accepts my excuses - but Mama
sends me a questioning look. I have avoided any
questions thus far, but I suspect La Madre will not give
up easily.

May 25

I spoke with Mama earlier today after a letter from
Edward arrived, asking me to return to Connaught
Place immediately. She knew something was amiss, and
I told her of my suspicions.

Her reaction shocked and embarrassed me - in equal
parts. She told me that men "being what they are" often
have "understandings" with women not their wives.
Aristocratic men especially often satisfy their "needs"

with women of a lower class. Even so, I do not even have actual proof of "an indiscretion," but as long as "genuine affection" continues in my marriage, my "suspicions should be forgotten." She told me that she would write to Edward telling him that I need a few weeks at home as a break from the hectic social season, but that I would return to London before summer.

It is not often that I am made speechless.

May 26

I know Mama's advice is practical, but my heart rebels against it.

May 30

We all will visit Holkham to see the newest member of the Coke family, Grandpapa's second son, another boy yet to be named. I look forward to seeing my boisterous extended family again. I have been silent in my own thoughts for too long.

Holkham Hall

Norfolk, England

June 4

Is there anything lovelier than the English countryside in June? After seeing step-mother Anne who looked pale, Grandpapa who looked proud, and Baby who, though pink and healthy, smelled most dreadfully, I escaped to ride the estate with my brothers. I tested my mare Molly by riding full gallop to inch past both Ed and Ken in a race to the shore. I doubt that I will be able to beat them much longer. Both of the boys have grown nearly as tall as Papa in the months since I have last seen them. Papa is again at sea, but I am glad for that - I would be ashamed for him to know of my troubled marriage. I am even uneasy in the company of Aunt Anne, from whom I know Mama keeps no secrets. She tells me that she will ask her son, George, to act as my escort in London, if Edward's schedule does not allow him to accompany me socially. However, neither George, nor his brother, Henry, are here. Henry continues his studies at Oxford, and George his work in Parliament. However, I am not without a male admirer at Holkham, Frederick Madden, a young scholar who

Grandpapa has hired to catalogue the many ancient manuscripts in his library. He follows my every move, and - to my shame - I do not discourage him.

June 10

Oh Marianne, whatever was I thinking? Well, thinking had little to do with what transpired between Frederick and me. Let me explain.

Frederick and I often meet before dinner to discuss his catalogues or perhaps a book I have been reading, sometimes we even take walks around the gardens. I find his company charming and his adoration a balm to my spirit. However nothing untoward had happened, until yesterday.

We had met as usual in the salon in the late afternoon. There I entertained him with my lute, singing Italian love songs that I learned at Tunbridge. But before leaving the salon for dinner he pulled me into his arms and kissed me thoroughly, as he murmured, *mi belle amore*. I did not protest.

During dinner he stared at me so longingly that I found myself blushing fiercely enough that Mama asked whether I had caught a chill. After dinner Frederick escorted me to my chambers where I invited him into . . . my bed. He was a sweet and gentle lover, but I regretted my decision shortly afterwards and asked him to leave.

My God, what have I done?

June 12

Mr. Madden hounds me, asking me repeatedly why I am "so cold" with him. I have no good response - until I confide in Eugenie who tells me how to rid myself of him. She advises telling him that, "I shall be required to tell my husband of your unwanted advances" if he persists. Her advice works. Poor man, he now avoids me. The French always seem to have the perfect answer to every question about love.

June 14

Edward has written asking for my forgiveness with a poem so sweet, so intimate that I cannot share it with you Marianne. I borrow a Holkham carriage and William, our former groom from Forston, to drive me to London tomorrow.

June 16

Edward's warm welcome has given me hope for our future. He proposed that we spend two weeks in Paris, a proposal I accepted eagerly. There I hope we can mend the tear in our marriage.

I am not with child.

June 22

For the third time in my life I travel across the English Channel. Last time I looked forward to an uncertain future. This time I cross to repair the past.

Paris, France

June 25

Edward and I are wary of one another as we tour Paris, as though we are acquaintances rather than lovers. We speak of the present - of the brilliant early summer weather as we walk the *Palais-Royal*, of the perfect specimen of rose in the *Jardin du Luxembourg*, of a certain slant of light over the city near sunset. He has not touched me except in casual contact - a touch of my elbow to help me into the carriage or a press of his knee as we sit side by side at *The Marriage of Figaro*. It is I that turns to him before bed. We gently explore one another - each angle, each curve is rediscovered. Our touches express what we cannot.

June 30

Eugenie and I explored old Paris today. Edward required a day for business matters (one day only, he promises, Marianne). However Eugenie, with her knowledge of *Ile de la Cite*, made for an excellent companion and tour guide. We arrived by the *Pont Neuf* bridge where we were unnerved by the mascarons, the grotesque stone masks that decorate its span. We admired the equestrian statue of Henry IV, the Green Gallant, which was damaged during the French Revolution but rebuilt after the fall of Napoleon. We then saw the *Conciergerie*, whose beautiful exterior hides dark dungeons below. Eugenie told me that Marie Antoinette, Madame du Barry, even Robespierre were held captive there before their executions by guillotine.

But by far the most interesting was *Notre-Dame de Paris*. The Gothic cathedral itself was magnificent with its flying buttresses, imposing bell towers and gabled portals, though much of its structure was destroyed and its treasures looted during the Revolution. This sad tale was told to us by an intriguing young man we met during our tour. With his tousled hair, brooding expression, and Gallic nose he was hardly handsome, though his expressive eyes were fierce as he asked us, *Puis-je vous aider?* He indeed helped us with his passionate denouncement of the wrongs done to his "Lady of Paris" during the Reign of Terror - a thirteenth century spire was torn down, statues were beheaded, tombs robbed, even the Virgin Mary was replaced on the altars by the "Goddess of Liberty." It was enough to boil even my Anglican blood! But the most troubling desecration, according to our companion, was the removal of the many stained glass windows, only the exquisite north and south rose windows remain. He said that some day soon he would write of his cathedral and perhaps then proper restorations would be completed. I asked him his name, so that I might read his work in the future. He replied, "Victor Hugo."

July 7

We return home to London tomorrow. As we return to our routines, I shall try to forget what Edward - and I - have done, but it is my misfortune to have a terribly good memory.

Connaught Place
London, England
July 12

We have been in London for less than a week, and the heat of summer is already upon us. And with that heat comes the - there is no delicate way to say it, Marianne - the stench of its over one million inhabitants. Men of medicine warn of the miasma, the bad air which brings disease. Those who can escape London do so. I leave for Roehampton tomorrow. Poor Edward must remain to conduct business and politics, but he will spend the coming weekends and most of August with me in our country home.

Elm Grove
Roehampton, England
July 20

I spend many of my weekdays riding *astride*. Are you
shocked? I have ridden astride for years with my
brothers, despite my mother's and Steely's objections.
But with the aid of the grooms I charmed at Forston
and Holkham, I was able to ride as I wished in secret.
There is nothing more exhilarating than riding at full
gallop, a gait impossible riding aside. The lady's side-
saddle is fine for an amble in Hyde Park, but a more
vigorous gait causes the saddle to slide most
alarmingly. However, chafing is an even more delicate
problem for the lady who rides astride. I have solved
this by wearing discarded breeches inexpertly but
sufficiently altered by me. I am both sneaky and clever,
am I not?

Here I am able to ride as I wish with the help of William
who is now one of our groomsmen at both Connaught
and Roehampton. Each morning he prepares Molly for
my daily ride, though I do not even need his assistance
in mounting her. What freedom! Eugenie warns me that

I risk injury to my "womanly parts," but I believe that to be a foolish superstition. Surely manly parts are much more likely to be damaged when riding!

Pardon my indelicacy, Marianne.

July 26

I am reading the most fascinating book, *Frankenstein* by Mary Shelley, the young widow of Percy Shelley, the poet and friend of Lord Byron. The story behind the novel is almost as interesting as the novel itself. In 1816, when staying in Geneva, she, her husband, and Byron competed in a story writing contest the three devised to while away the long, rainy days of a summer holiday. She won with her story about a mad doctor and a reanimated corpse which later became her novel. She based the story upon Giovanni Aldini who experimented upon the body of an executed murderer, George Foster, by attempting to reanimate his body with electricity. The true experiment, according to what I have read, had limited success, but the fictional one much more so. In the imagination of Mrs. Shelley a reanimated monster is born. How gruesome . . . how wonderful!

Steely would never have allowed me to read such a book.

August 7

My days, and nights, have been spent with Edward, who has finally joined me at Roehampton. We walk the gardens. We ride (he astride, me aside) the acres. We dine alone. On occasion we invite neighbours to play whisk. He spoils me with another trip to Brighton. We sleep late - one body curled against the other. I wish we could remain so.

August 18

Edward grows distant of late. I can see he is eager to return to London, to a life of which I am only one small part.

Connaught Place
London, England
September 2

We have returned to London. Edward and I return to our routines - I to domestic mismanagement, he to politics and debate.

I have written Forston to invite Steely and her sister Jane for a lengthy visit, so that we may visit and tour the city together. I look forward to seeing my old friends.

I am not with child.

September 16

Our first anniversary has come and gone. I gave Edward a Lever gold pocket watch; he gave me a lovely necklace of diamonds reset from his family's jewels. We then dined at Simpson's Tavern. Potted shrimp in butter to start, followed by steak and kidney pie, and custard tart for dessert.

Am I too young to wear diamonds, Marianne?

September 30

Steely and Jane have arrived! It is so very nice to be able to natter about anything with those one has known from childhood. We all speak our minds and unfortunately the subject turns to children, or, in my case, the absence of them. Steely tells me to wait for the full moon to conceive. Jane suggests I wear rose quartz. Both warn me to never sit on cold stone. Such helpful fertility advice from maiden ladies!

October 7

I took Steely and Jane to tour two of London landmarks. How odd it is that I never thought to visit Westminster Abbey or the Tower before. We Londoners do take for granted the history that lies at our doorstep.

Site of the coronations of all British monarchs since William the Conqueror, Westminster is a magnificent Gothic structure that inspired much awe in my guests, daughters of a humble clergyman. King Edward's Chair, the massive oak chair where our royalty are crowned, was their particular favourite. I preferred the Poet's

Corner, where great writers such as Geoffrey Chaucer, Edmund Spenser, and Lord Byron are buried or memorialized.

All three of us were amazed by the Tower of London, which is both a prison and an attraction for the curious with shillings to spare. We ignored the various artilleries and armouries on display (please don't tell Papa) and spent our shillings on the Royal Menagerie, where over sixty stone beasts make their home. We also enjoyed the tour of the Jewel-office where the Royal Jewels are kept. Even so, our imaginations provided us with the most memorable encounter, the Tower Green, the place of many dreadful executions, including the beheading of Anne Boleyn. We all agreed that she was treated most unfairly by Henry VIII. Her headless ghost is said to haunt the Tower to this very day.

October 15

Steely and Jane departed yesterday. I find my days hard to fill.

October 20

I have just received word from Mama that Papa is home, for convalescence from the malaria. I leave for Forston tomorrow.

Edward remains in London.

Forston House

Dorset, England

October 22

It is so very difficult to see my darling Babou in such a state. His fever has produced the most dreadful symptoms. He shivers and sweats. He complains of headache and of belly cramps. He calls out for Mama, then a moment later appears not to know her. We all fear he may die, Marianne.

October 30

Thank God. Papa is already on the mend. A tonic made of fever tree bark mixed with gin has improved his symptoms, not to mention his mood, considerably. He now complains of boredom, but has been ordered by La Madre to remain in bed. I entertain him by reading aloud Sir Walter Scott's latest novel, *The Talisman*, or I play guitar and sing. He asks me whether I should return home to my husband. I tell him that I will as soon as he is well, that Edward does not need me.

Later he asks me, "Are you happy, Janie?"

"Of course," I respond.

"You know, your mother and I only want the best for you."

"I know, Papa. I know."

Is my discontent so obvious?

November 8

I leave for London tomorrow. Papa is now well, so well that he orders all of us about - until Mama sweetly reminds him that he is not aboard ship.

Connaught Place

London, England

November 30

Since I have returned to London, I have thought long
about my marriage, about Edward's hours spent in his
work, about my growing restlessness.

I attempted to broach the subject with him last night
after dinner, his first with me in over a week. He
listened for a moment and quickly identified the
problem. I was bored, a problem easily solved. The
Christmas season was almost upon us. We would spend
time together at Roehampton and at Holkham. After
that, perhaps a dinner party or two until the season
starts. Problem solved.

How can difficulties in a marriage be discussed when
only one partner sees them?

December 7

I have asked Edward to allow me the funds to have a conservatory constructed for our home in Roehampton. If boredom be the problem, a building project is the answer. He has agreed, reluctantly - no doubt thinking another necklace or bauble a more convenient Christmas gift to bestow upon me. I however look forward to having a warm and sunny greenhouse to enjoy the winter months. I shall begin sketching my retreat immediately!

December 15

I have spent the last week leaning over my sketchpad. My posture may never be the same, Marianne, but I am finally satisfied with my effort. My conservatory is based upon the one at Holkham. Although much smaller than Holkham's, my conservatory extends off the east wing for morning sun and afternoon shade with a gabled roof and lattice windows from floor to ceiling. I plan to have an informal sitting area and a small area for a winter garden. I cannot wait to show Edward my plans.

Elm Grove

Roehampton, England

December 18

Edward and I arrived earlier today to meet with the architect, a young student of the great Robert Smirke, who will build the conservatory here. Edward thought it best that a professional create the plans and supervise the construction, particularly since such an addition to our home should reflect well upon us. Edward wishes for a much larger space for the conservatory with ample room for dining and an orangery. Mr. Underwood will prepare the initial drawings for approval in a few days.

December 22

Edward approved Mr. Underwood's drawing for the conservatory. They hope to begin construction by early spring.

I am sure it will be quite impressive, but frankly, I wanted something less impressive but even more important - a place of my own.

Holkham Hall
Norfolk, England
December 24

Merry Christmas, Marianne! Edward and I spend the entire holiday week at Holkham. Snow has arrived, as if cued by a theatrical director. It began falling shortly after we arrived and now covers the estate grounds with a thick blanket. My young cousins burn their letters to St. Nicholaus over the yule log, while the adults dip their cups into the wassail bowl. The combination of the fire and the mulled ale warm us all.

December 27

While Edward talks politics with Papa and Grandpapa, Mama and Auntie Anne talk of children and childbirth with their stepmother. Grandpapa's Anne is expecting, *again.* I spend much of my time with my brothers and my cousin, Henry, who I join sledding and ice skating. Henry will soon complete his studies at Oxford and plans to tour not only Europe but also Greece and Syria after he graduates. How I envy him! Cousin George, who is far too mature for our games, teases me about

my tomboy ways whenever he sees me, calling me
Madame Hoyden. I respond by telling him that perhaps
he could teach me better manners, as his mother has
suggested escorting me in London.

He answers with a sly smile, "Perhaps I shall, little
cousin."

1827

Connaught Place

London, England

January 5

We have returned to London with the new year. Edward is again to Parliament, while I fill the days with my art and music. We have been invited by Prince and Princess Esterhazy to a dinner party later in the month, a welcomed diversion until the season begins.

January 21

What I had hoped would be a diversion turned disastrous last night.

Our evening began pleasantly enough. It was good to see our friends from Almack's, but after dinner as the women followed the Princess for tea in the drawing room, I overheard Lady Holland, a formidable gossip, whisper to a companion that Edward continues his affair with the confectioner's daughter. Her companion urged her to lower her voice to which the lady responded, "It is best she knows of her husband."

I remember little else of the evening.

January 22

I confronted Edward this morning with Lady Holland's claim. He denied it, saying that she has never disguised her dislike for him, and that she continually seeks drama and will create it where she cannot find it.

I do not believe him.

March 5

The London season begins with a *riotto* in masquerade at Almack's. I wear a black velvet gown with decolletage to better display the diamond necklace given to me by Edward. However, Edward is not in attendance. His work once again takes precedence. No matter. I intend to enjoy the evening with or without him. Behind a mask, a lady can enjoy considerable freedoms. I travel by carriage with only William, our groom, as escort. I dance with countless men whose faces I cannot see and whose voices I cannot identify - until I hear one familiar. George Anson asks me for this dance, a waltz. He holds me more tightly than he should, as we circle the room in three-quarter time. His breath teases my ear, as he asks whether we might meet sometime later, somewhere more private. I am silent until the music stops, when I suggest meeting at my carriage on the corner of King Street, St. James. "Follow me in five minutes," I say. I do not wait for his answer, but instead walk quickly from the crowded ballroom towards my carriage where I ask Will to return in one hour. I wait and watch for George. I soon see him, standing beneath the street lamp bathed in its light. I open the door and softly call out his name. "Hello, little cousin," he whispers. "We have only one hour," I answer. He smiles and says, "Only one?"

March 6

Little more than a day has passed since the *riotto*, and already he writes to me to ask when we will meet again. Oh Marianne, I know I should hesitate. I should consider my reputation. I should see Steely's disapproving looks, the hurt I may cause Mama and Papa. I should think of Edward - though he rarely thinks of me.

I should, but I shall not.

Instead, I see George's warm brown eyes looking down at me, feel his lips upon my breast. His hands follow the curve of my back, as we join hip-to-hip and move to a rhythm of our own making.

March 10

George and I are to Roehampton for the day with Edward's blessing.

I told my husband of my cousin's willingness to escort me when Edward's schedule in Parliament prevents him from doing so. He did not think to question how George, who is also a member of Parliament, finds time for me. He instead encourages us to inspect the progress with the conservatory. We agreed to do so - with enthusiasm.

March 30

Apologies, Marianne. Like a fickle friend, I ignore you when a man pays court to me. Every Wednesday I meet George at Almack's. We are so discreet that even the gossip mongers there are not suspicious of us. We are cousins, after all! Other days of the week we just happen to meet - with the assistance of Will and Eugenie - at Hyde Park, or we take another day trip to Roehampton, entering a side door, so as to not disturb the servants. I am thinking perhaps a trip to Brighton may be in order when the weather warms.

April 3

Another birthday. My twentieth. I awoke to an apologetic note from Edward who writes that he must leave early for work but promises to take me to the theatre tonight, where I can wear the lovely sapphire necklace with matching earrings he has given me. I wonder how I shall fill my day?

I meet him in the afternoon at his rooms on Regency. We spend hours in bed, enjoying the luxury of time with no purpose, except one.

I admire the long line of his back, the neat curve of backside. As he turns to me, he sighs long and low and murmurs, "My beautiful cousin." I run my hand over the reddish curls on his chest, tracing the line of them over the soft flesh of his belly to the hardness below. "My beautiful cousin," I reply. His slender fingers, so like my own, stroke my neck, breast, belly, and between.

Brighton

Sussex, England

April 16

George and I have arrived at the Norfolk Hotel in Brighton to take the sea air for a few days. All is quite proper, of course. Edward gave his approval, and we have taken separate rooms. The weather is unseasonably warm for April. Perhaps I can convince George to swim with me later.

We swam naked under a moonless night. The water was cold, but we were not.

Connaught Place
London, England
April 20

Darling, dear, dearest, love, lover, sweetheart. We say the words but never speak to them. *Later, to come, coming, following, future?* We speak only of the past or present.

April 24

I believe I am with child, Marianne.

Jhrujh pxvw eh wkh idwkhu.

April 25

I slip naked from my bed not long after Great Tom, Westminster's bell tower, chimes midnight. I walk to his door, opening it quietly. With only a half moon to light my way, I carefully approach his bed. I whisper, "Edward." He responds with a voice hoarse with sleep, "Janet?" I do not answer, but instead pull down the quilt to join him. "What a surprise," he says. "A pleasant one?" I ask as I stroke his hair, chin, chest . . . and beyond. "Far more than pleasant, my dear."

How to Seduce Your Husband.

April 27

I tell no one of my suspicions, Marianne. I'll wait until next month - to be sure.

Today is Tuesday, the day I typically go to confession. I shall go no longer. I cannot confess my sins. And even if I could, I'll not confess to what I shall not do without.

May 2

George and I attended May Day at Westminster with Mama and Papa yesterday. We shared gossip about family and friends amid the children dancing around the Maypole. We tried to make ourselves heard above the click-clack of sticks and the jingle-jangle of bells from the Moorish dancers who, with Jack-in-the-Green, begged for pennies to pay for the feasting later. George told us that his brother Henry is soon to graduate Oxford and leave for his Grand Tour through Europe and onto Arabia. How wonderful to have the freedom to see the world! I thought back to our days at Holkham and how far away they now seem.

Later we watched the Queen and King of May crowned. George joked about the "green marriages" of couples who spend the night together in the forest, saying we could expect the number of births in London to increase in nine months time. Papa laughed, Mama acted shocked and said, "How you talk, George." I remained curiously silent.

May 30

I could wait no longer. I have told him. He asked whether I was sure. I told him I was sure that I am - and that he is the father.

I saw doubt in his eyes, Marianne.

June 10

Lord and Lady Ellenborough have made it known to family and a small circle of friends that they expect the birth of their first child early next year.

June 18

Edward and I attended Almack's, thinking to celebrate
our good news. Instead I saw George dancing with
Isabelle Forster, a very pretty debutante. They looked
at each other with such affection that even Edward
noticed and commented on George's "new conquest."

Off with the old, on with the new.

June 25

Edward has suggested that we spend two weeks in
Brighton early next month. I suggested someplace new
for us, the Isle of Wight. To my surprise, he agreed.
Since I have made known to him my interesting
condition, he is eager to please me

Isle of Wight, England

July 5

It is good to escape London. I feared the crossing of the Channel might prove disastrous to my delicate stomach, but my sickness has fortunately eased in the past week, as has my moodiness. I am determined to live in the present and look only to the future.

Although the Isle is less than a day's journey from London, it is as though we have travelled to a place otherworldly. Edward and I stay at a small inn near the village of Shanklin Chine, where we follow a footpath through a coastal ravine, where we pass lush greenery and a small stream that ends at a cascading waterfall. Continuing on a fisherman's path, we arrive at the shoreline, where we play keep away from the constant waves that rush to soak our bare feet. Later we walk onto the forest of fossils with its remnants of ancient trees and see on the sandstone ledges strange bones and footprints of what must have been an enormous lizard.

The salt air and ocean breeze are a balm to my troubled mind and, I hope, to our troubled marriage.

July 15

We saw Carisbrooke Castle today, our last day before
we return to London. Although originally built as a
defensive castle by the Earl of Devon, Baldwin de
Redvers, in the early 12th century, it is better known as
the prison of Charles I, who remained there under
house arrest until his execution during the Civil War.
Now it is used occasionally by the island's militia, but is
more frequently visited by curious sightseers such as
ourselves. As with most Norman castles, the many
years have taken their toll. Though the twin turrets and
entryway are still magnificent, much of the stonework
is crumbling.

Edward and I strolled its lawn hand-in-hand in
companionable silence. I had hoped to see
Carisbrooke's grey lady, the notorious ghost who roams
the grounds with her dogs and a man dressed in a
brown jerkin - or to see the face of Elizabeth Ruffin in
the castle's well. She, according to legend, fell into the
well and tragically drowned. Many claim to see her face
floating on the water's surface. However I saw nothing.
Perhaps I have not inherited my parent's familiarity
with the spirit world. Edward saw nothing either, but

then he wouldn't, since he does not believe in ghosts -
or in being haunted.

Elm Grove
Roehampton, England
July 22

Since our return from the Isle of Wight, Edward is
staying in London for his work, while I stay at
Roehampton. And although I have had many visitors -
Edward's sister, Elizabeth, just paid a call yesterday -
and I still attend dinner parties hosted by close friends
and relatives, I find my world getting smaller and
smaller.

I try not to think too far ahead, but my body keeps
reminding me of the event to come. I am eating more,
gaining weight. I'll soon be as plump as Mama. My
breasts are swelling. My nose is often congested, my
gums often sore. My face is in continual blush. Eugenie
tells me that these changes are normal, that she
experienced them in her pregnancy as well, but in
addition sprouted hairs upon her chin.

I suppose I shall need to keep tweezers handy.

August 1

I have received the most dreadful news, Marianne.

Late yesterday morning, I received an unexpected visit - from George Anson. I could tell immediately that something was frightfully wrong. He told me he had just received word that his brother and my dear cousin, Henry, died in Syria during his Grand Tour. He and his classmate, John Fox Strangways, were arrested in Aleppo after entering a mosque dressed as Muslims, though they failed to remove their shoes, according to Islamic custom. This breach in conduct angered onlookers who attacked them. Henry and John were then placed in prison, where they remained in squalid conditions until diplomatic actions released them. Unfortunately both young men had contracted the plague in prison. Our poor Henry died just outside Aleppo before medical help could be found.

George was so overcome with the telling of his tragic news that he began to cry quietly with his head in hands, his shoulders heaving with each intake of breath. I went to him and held him as we wept.

Connaught Place
London, England
November 15

I have neglected you for months, Marianne. Since news of Henry's death, I have found it difficult to put thought to paper. His death and my fears couple to produce an anxiety I cannot shake. Each morning I rise determined to see Henry as a lost friend gone before and to take solace in the new life to come, but that determination slowly erodes. Even so, I continue on.

Mama and Edward agreed that my lying-in should take place in London, as is the custom among the fashionable. Here at Connaught a suite of rooms have been prepared so that family and friends might visit mother and child during their confinement. An *accoucheur* has been hired to assist with the birth. A nursemaid and wet-nurse have been retained.

I wait.

November 30

Papa has given me a copy of *The Private Memoirs of Kenelm Digby*, a newly published account of our illustrious (and notorious) ancestor's life, to combat the boredom of my confinement. Philosopher, scientist, diplomat, pirate, and namesake to my dear little brother, Kenelm, was an extraordinary man. He was envoy for King Charles I, a friend to Descartes. He sailed the Mediterranean Sea and invented the wine bottle. But best of all, he loved the beautiful Venetia Stanley, whose early (and suspicious) death he mourned most desperately. Eugenie tells me that some censored portions of the memoir are being circulated around London. I wonder what *they* may contain, Marianne!

December 29

Lord and Lady Ellenborough announce the birth of their first child, a boy - to be named Charles Dudley Law.

1828

Connaught Place

London, England

January 10

The birth was an easy one. Both Mama and my *accoucheur*, Sir William Kingston, have deemed it so, though I doubt any woman new from childbed recalls her lying-in as easy. I have been told that the pain is soon forgotten, though I cannot imagine how the memory of such pain could disappear.

Wave upon wave. Cramping. Twisting. Burning. Stabbing. Hour after hour. Pushing. Screaming until hoarse.

The child arrives. A cry not my own. Big head. No neck. Short legs. Blue hands and feet. Whispers. Sir William.

Mama. Papa. Edward. One more push. Utter exhaustion. Oblivion.

My darling boy.

January 12

Charles is delicate. He is reluctant to feed, despite the best efforts of his wet-nurse and cries most incessantly, according to his nursemaid. Nevertheless, he is adored. His grandparents make much fuss over him, and Edward is very proud. He has already made plans for Charles's christening and has asked the Duke of Wellington and Princess Esterhazy to be his godparents. Both have agreed.

January 28

I quickly regain my health, though Charles fails to thrive, so much so that his baptism was held in our home to avoid exposing the darling boy to the winter's chill. My parents, Steely, Auntie Anson, Edward's sister, Elizabeth, and his godparents were in attendance. Edward's uncle, the Bishop of Bath, performed the ceremony.

February 18

Such a mix of good and bad news, Marianne. Edward has been appointed Lord Privy Seal by our new Prime Minister, the Duke of Wellington. Sir William has said that I may resume normal activities, including "relations." Unfortunately, he finds Charles's health still frail and recommends that he spend the next few months at Roehampton with his nurses, away from the city's bad air. Edward and I must remain at Connaught Place for his new appointment and the coming social season.

March 10

An embassy ball begins the new social season - and a new Tory Government.

A new tradition borrowed from Vienna is created to help the ladies in attendance remember dances promised. A dance card is issued where they may record the names of the gentlemen; however, the gentlemen must still rely on their memories!

Lady Ellenborough's Dance Card (First Set):

1. My Lord Ellenborough is my partner for the evening's first dance, a quadrille. We dance its figures with three other couples, including the Duke of Wellington and his partner, Lady Jersey. Her attempts to charm him seem to have met with little success.
2. A Scottish Reel with Sir Robert Peel, the Home Secretary and the Duke's right arm man. His energy more than makes up for his lack of footwork, as my trampled toes will confirm.
3. A Waltz with Count Lieven. Dear Christopher is, as always, a man of few words - a quality I suppose developed from his marriage to a woman of many.
4. I dance the Polanaise with Prince Felix Schwarzenberg to whom Princess Esterhazy introduced me earlier in the evening. He dances, like most men from the Continent, most gracefully - take note men of Britain. He is also my dinner partner.

Dinner and Intermission - The Prince makes for a charming dinner companion. As is tradition for formal affairs, the gentlemen serve the ladies. Felix, as he demands I call him, makes certain that I receive the best the banquet offers. As we dine on Chateaubriand Steak he speaks of his family home in Bohemia. Over a dessert of Banbury cakes I speak of Holkham Hall. He is quite possibly the most elegant man I have ever encountered, impeccably dressed with great moustaches. His every movement is measured, his every word carefully chosen. Only his magnetic eyes hint at an awareness unspoken.

Second Set:

1. A Cotillion with Viscount Melbourne, Secretary to Ireland. His first public appearance since his father's and his wife's death earlier this year. Poor man.
2. Foreign Secretary, John Ward, the Earl of Dudley and second godfather to my sweet Charlie. Another Reel. He speaks of nothing more than the latest cricket match at *Lord's*.
3. Another dance, a Viennese Waltz this time, with Prince Schwarzenberg. As we make the quick turns, his eyes never leave my face. His intensity causes me to ask, "What are you staring at, Sir?" His reply? "Why at you, Madame."
4. My husband claims the last dance, another Waltz, with me. Could he be jealous of the attention paid to me by the Prince? Unlikely.

March 11

I met the Prince while riding in Hyde Park earlier today. As we rode Rotten Row together enjoying the warmth of the spring sun and the sweet smell of daffodil and hyacinth blossoms, I remarked upon our chance meeting. He replied, "Chance had nothing to do with our meeting, Jane."

March 12

A bouquet of daffodils arrived today with a card that read, "Meet me at Almack's this Wednesday."

March 15

I convinced Edward to attend Almack's with me last night. I polanaissed with the Prince who told me that he will be sure to be more specific with his requests of me next time. "Next time?" I replied.

March 16

Today I had tea with Princess Esterhazy who spoke to me of Prince Schwarzenberg - in the strictest confidence, of course. She said that he has spoken of me to all the Patronesses of Almack's. "He is infatuated with you, my dear." To which I replied, "I am flattered, but not interested."

Did I lie, Marianne?

Elm Grove
Roehampton, England
March 18

I have left London to see my darling boy. His nursemaids tell me he is improving daily, though he is still frail. And I am still reluctant to hold him, though he grins toothless and sweet when I do. My lack of maternal instinct troubles me, though I am not surprised. As a girl I rarely bothered with baby dolls, or baby cousins for that manner, preferring instead the company of my brothers or the menagerie of animals to be found at Forston and Holkham. Still, one would think a child of one's own would be different.

Texq fp tolkd tfqe jb, Jxofxkkb?

March 20

I feel like I am hiding here at Elm Grove, playing some odd game of hide and seek with myself, trying to discover my real wants and needs. I want to love my husband and my child, but cannot. But I need to love and be loved.

Tomorrow I leave for London - still uncertain.

Connaught Place
London, England
March 23

I have not been home for more than a day when a letter arrives from the Prince. Here are its contents:

My dearest Jane,

I am told by the Countess that you have left London without notice for your country home in Roehampton. I suspect that I am the reason for this sudden departure. Forgive me if my attentions have been unwanted. I will desist at once if indeed that is the case. Yet I cannot help think my regard, my desire . . . my love for you might be returned, if only you would give me the chance to show the depth of my feelings. They should not be measured by the briefness of our acquaintance. I propose that we meet next Wednesday at 9 in the evening, not at Almack's, not with your husband, but *alone* at my rooms at 23 Knightsbridge. I wait impatiently, hopefully, expectantly, my darling.

F. S.

March 26

A dozen white roses were delivered today. No card.

March 27

A dozen pink roses. No card.

March 28

A dozen red roses. One card, one word. *Tomorrow.*

March 29

I went to him tonight, Marianne. I can recall each word and gesture distinctly, as though I am still there, standing before him.

"I didn't think you would come," he said.

"I almost didn't," I confessed.

He smiled and asked, "Would you like tea, or wine, perhaps?"

"No," I replied as I moved closer to him. He looked into my eyes and pulled me even closer, leaning down to kiss my lips - at first soft and tender, then firm and unwavering. Minutes later our lips part, and he asked whether we should retire to his bedchambers. I said that we should. There he undressed me slowly and completely. First unbuttoning my dress, then untying my stays, until I was naked before him. I slipped under the bed linens and watched as he quickly undressed, leaving his clothes in a pile upon the floor near mine. I saw that he was as eager for me as I was for him.

Rapture. I had been too long without.

April 3

My twenty-first birthday.

April 6

I wake every morning and fall asleep every night to thoughts of him. In between, I plan ways to meet with him or wait impatiently for word from him.

He says that I have bewitched him. I wish it were true, that I could cast a spell upon him, bind him to me evermore.

April 14

I thought I had loved Edward once, but now I see that I only imagined myself so. I was a child flattered by the attentions of a man much older than I. He thought he loved me, I suppose. I wanted to love him.

I thought I had loved George, the object of a childish infatuation. Our affair was as inevitable as a summer rain, and as intense and brief.

But my love for Felix is not the love of a child. I love him as a woman loves a man, he as a man loves a woman. Our love believes and hopes all things.

April 22

Our love makes us brazen. We meet at Almack's. At Hyde Park. The Patronesses send us disapproving looks. The *haul ton* whisper as we pass them on Rotten Row. Will, my groom, drives me to 73 Harley Street, just a few doors down from my parent's townhouse, where Felix now takes rooms. We can now meet nearly every day, though with Mama and Steely in London, I suppose we should be more discreet.

May 15

A most curious incident occurred between my Prince and George Anson the other day at the Derby. It is not surprising that we chanced upon George at the tracks, since he has raised racing horses for some years. Even less surprising is that some jealous animosity emerged between my old lover and my new. George told us one of his horses, Colonel, was to run the first race. Hearing this, Felix said that he would then place a bet on Colonel's stiffest competition, Cadland. This rather rude declaration was not lost on my cousin who became even more angry when Cadland easily trounced Colonel for first prize.

Now the gossips of Almack's have taken to calling Felix, Cadland, because he beat out *Colonel* Anson, not only at the tracks but at love as well! Who am I to dispute that, Marianne?

May 21

A novel has been written about Almack's, a *roman a clef*, a thinly veiled account of the scandals and dramas of the fashionable in their favourite social club. It is called, appropriately enough, *Almack's*, and the author has chosen to remain anonymous. And most amusing of all - I am one of its characters! Of course I had to find a copy to see my "fictional" characterization, Lady Glenmore, for myself. Unfortunately, Lady Glenmore, though beautiful, is only a minor character and says very little - so much for truth in fiction!

June 1

Today Steely lectured me concerning my reputation. At first I thought she may have learned of my affair with Felix, but to my relief, she and Mama have heard only of the publication of *Almack's* and my portrayal in it. I protested that I have done nothing wrong, that I cannot be responsible for what others write. Steely told me that a family member, a wife of one of my many cousins, is responsible for penning *Almack's*. It seems *her* lack of discretion counts for little, but *my* behaviour for much.

Let them grumble, I say.

Elm Grove
Roehampton, England
June 15

I have escaped London and all its unpleasantness. The
bad air and soot. My husband's coolness. My family's
meddling.

My sweet Charlie. The nursemaids tell me that he has
started teething and fusses so dreadfully that they rub
his gums with brandy to calm him. I shall have a coral
gum stick made for my poor darling.

My Prince and I have made a pact to meet in secret
every Thursday here at Elm Grove. Three days until I
see his face, hear his voice, and feel his touch.

June 19

Our first lover's tryst. I have given Felix a key to the
little used entrance at Elm Grove so that he might come
and go undetected. The daring intrigue adds to our
mutual seduction. Here we revel in our privacy. Here I

can imagine Felix and I as man and wife - as the husband I should have.

June 26

This week we ride with the help of Will who makes ready Molly and Felix's mount. Felix is rather shocked that I choose to ride astride, but enjoys the gallops that are made possible with my choice. During our exploration of Elm Grove's acres we come upon an abandoned cottage where we stop for a picnic of cheese and wine. The sweet fragrance of late blooming roses drifts over us as we make love upon green grass.

June 27

I have enlisted the aid of Eugenie and Will to make ready the cottage Felix and I found for next Thursday. Some minor repairs and cleaning, curtains for the windows, a new pallet and bedding, a borrowed barn cat for the mice, and flowers for the kitchen table should make for a cozy retreat.

July 3

We are more than the love we make. We are companions of the mind and heart. We talk of music, art, poetry, books - and though he is a diplomat he never speaks of politics, never voices an opinion on the issues of the day. As we lie upon the pallet with limbs intertwined, we listen to the soft rain outside. Felix asks me how we might make a future together. Divorce is an impossibility, even our King could not escape the bonds of an unhappy marriage. We speak of running away to the north country, to an inn he has heard of near Richmond Castle. But how can we risk sacrificing our reputations and that of our families, Marianne? And if not, how can our love survive?

July 10

Today, instead of meeting with my Prince, I must welcome Edward home for his return from Parliament. For two weeks I must play devoted wife to a man I no longer love.

July 24

I have refused Edward his marital right. I will not subject you to a description of the unpleasant scene that ensued but, needless to say, he was angry - as angry as I have ever seen him. He has left Elm Grove to return to London, perhaps to meet with his new mistress, an Italian countess, or so I've been told.

I care not.

July 28

I had word sent to Felix about my argument with Edward and his departure - asking him to take care, that I do not believe my husband knows of our affair, but that he should be on his guard nevertheless.

Now today word arrives from Felix in Richmond. He asks me to meet him at The King's Head Inn. I leave today.

Richmond

North Yorkshire, England

August 1

We are posing as husband and wife, travellers seeking to tour the most romantic castle in England and its surrounding countryside. What a lovely fantasy, but one in which I find difficult to indulge. The ruins of the great stone castle and the quaint medieval market in Richmond provide only momentary diversions. I keep thinking of my abandonment of sweet Charlie, my leaving without word to anyone. If news of my flight reaches my family, I can only imagine their worry. My thoughts even turn to Edward - he will worry too. After all, we did love one another once.

I tell Felix that I will return to Elm Grove. He can say and do nothing to change my mind.

Elm Grove
Roehampton, England
August 3

My feeble hope to escape detection was dashed
immediately upon my arrival. Edward and my parents
awaited me. I bore Edward's reproaches, Mama's tears,
and Papa's silence. I apologised for worrying them,
though I refused to tell them where, and to whom, I had
gone.

August 5

Mama and Papa have negotiated with Edward to
salvage our marriage. He has agreed to a reconciliation
with one condition - I shall no longer see, speak, or
even write to "that man" again.

My will is spent. I agree, to my shame.

November 15

We are husband and wife in name only. I rattle about
Elm Grove - with only the servants - who watch my

every step with veiled eyes - as company, while Edward pursues his endless fascination with politics and debate. My only pleasure is Charlie, who is now as chubby as a Botticelli cherub.

I dream of my Prince. I see him come to me. He gathers me in his arms and tells me to believe in our love - though I know I only write a story that I can read when I awake.

Holkham Hall

Kent, England

December 25

Edward and I have joined my family for Christmas. No recriminations, though I see curious appraisals. I hear whispered remarks. My family speaks to me only when I initiate conversation, when I enter a room conversation stops. Only my brothers and my Grandpapa treat me as Jane, perhaps they have not been told about the infidelity of Lady Ellenborough.

I remember once hearing about a strange custom among German Anabaptists called shunning, in which an errant member is denied social contact in punishment for open disregard of acceptable behaviour. A powerful custom, Marianne.

1829

Connaught Place

London, England

January 2

Edward and I have returned to Connaught Place in time for the opening session of Parliament. At least I will not be alone. I have Charlie who is now healthy enough to join us in London.

I look for Felix every corner I turn. He is never there.

January 3

Lord and Lady Londonderry - Edward's first wife's parents, if you forget, Marianne - have invited us to a masquerade ball next week with a Renaissance theme - perhaps I shall go as Henry VIII's fifth wife, Catherine

Howard, though I fear few would get the joke and even fewer would find it amusing.

January 10

At the ball I learned from Count Rodolphe Apponyi, Felix's friend and fellow diplomat, that my Prince still loves me despite my ill treatment of him. Oh Marianne, there is still hope!

January 11

I travel to 73 Harley Street by closed chaise driven by Will. Wearing a bonnet and veil as precaution against prying eyes, I quickly exit the carriage and climb the three steps to his door. His housekeeper answers my knock, and I wait nervously in the foyer while she announces my call. Moments later Felix appears. "Forgive me," I whisper. He doesn't answer. Instead he moves to me, and unties the strings of my bonnet, veil, and cloak and casts them aside. He then removes the combs from my hair, letting my hair fall to my shoulders. "My Jane," he finally says, looking into my eyes. He then takes my hand and leads me upstairs to his bedroom, where we become one and begin again.

February 1

I go to him three, sometimes four times a week. I steal away each time. I fear each time may be our last.

Brighton

Sussex, England

February 7

I have just arrived at **Norfolk Hotel** en route to Roehampton after a short visit to Forston to show off my pretty Charlie who is so much healthier now despite the nasty winter weather. I shall write to Edward to inform him of our safe arrival.

Felix is to arrive later by hired chariot. We shall spend our first night together in weeks!

February 8

Our tryst has been discovered by the night porter, an awful man named Robert Hepple who took it upon himself to spy upon us last night after seeing Felix enter my room late last night. This gentleman (if such a form of address should be used for such a man!) related the shameful details to Norfolk's proprietor who in turn related his account to me. I cannot tell you who was more embarrassed, Mr. Walton or me, by the details exposed. I pleaded with him to remain silent and gave him twenty pounds to assure that silence. Now I must tell Felix over breakfast.

Oh Marianne, if word reaches London, what will become of us?

Connaught Place

London, England

February 15

My worst fears have been made all too real. Edward has
received a letter from Mr. Hepple telling him of what he
saw and heard at the Norfolk Hotel. Although I
admitted to seeing Felix at the hotel, I denied the affair.
To my surprise, Edward appears to accept my
explanation, but I fear his acceptance will be short-
lived.

February 20

Yesterday morning I went looking for you in my desk,
only to find you missing, Marianne. At first I thought I
simply misplaced you in a spell of absent-mindedness,
but Eugenie and I combed my bedroom, my sitting
room, the library, even the dining room, but to no avail.
Later you magically materialised in my desk drawer. I
do not suspect Eugenie, since she would hardly be
foolish enough to return you to one of the places we
searched so carefully, but clearly someone "borrowed"
you. But who? One of the servants? But why? Has
Edward asked one of them to do so because he suspects

that I lied about the Prince? If so, how much was read? Just the thought of someone reading my innermost thoughts and emotions fills me with a sense of betrayal - and dread. I must be more circumspect. I shall keep you under lock and key, especially now.

F prpmbzq F xj mobdkxkq.

February 22

I have told Felix of my suspicions, all of them. He is as conflicted as I, both hopeful and worried for our future. He suggests caution until I am sure. I cannot think, so he must think for both of us.

March 25

We spent the month in limbo. We met in secret when we could, but our time together was uneasy with the waiting.

I am now as sure as I can be. I am with child.

March 30

Felix has consulted his ambassador concerning our predicament. Much to my distress, Prince and Princess Esterhazy have suggested his transfer to the embassy in Paris, fearing both a diplomatic disaster and the ruin of Felix's career when the scandal is made public. How little is their regard for me, and to think I considered both the Prince and Princess trusted friends!

April 3

My twenty-second birthday.

April 10

The decision has been made. Felix will join the embassy in Paris later this year. What shall we do?

May 11

I managed to see Felix off earlier today. He suggests that I ask Edward to allow me to go abroad without telling him that I am with child. Once abroad Felix would take care of me and our unborn child. We could finally be together, Marianne!

Elm Grove
Roehampton, England
May 24

I have taken refuge here at Elm Grove after another dreadful argument with Edward. I did as my Prince proposed and asked that I be allowed to go abroad "to consider my future" - to which Edward replied that under no circumstances would he allow me to leave England. I then, seeing no other choice, revealed that I am with child, that Felix is the father, and that I would not live without him. Edward's silence to my assertions was even more frightening than his anger. He finally said that he needed time to consider his recourses and demanded that I come here to Roehampton. He told me that he would have Mama and Steely accompany me.

So here we are, a miserable threesome awaiting my husband's decision - and I my future.

June 1

After consulting his solicitors, Edward suggests that we formally separate and that I, with my mother and Steely, rent a cottage in Ilfracombe to await the birth of the child.

I have no choice but to agree. I have heard no word from my Prince - I suspect his letters are being kept from me.

Ilfracombe

Devon, England

June 15

We have settled in here at a small cottage by the coast.
Unfortunately the sea offers me no solace.

I have still received no word from Felix, though I have
taken to retrieving the post before the servants do. I
have even asked Eugenie to send a letter that I have
written to Felix to his family home in Vienna. I trust
neither Mama nor Steely or any of the other servants.
As determined as they are to keep Felix and I apart, I
am equally determined to find a way for our love.

June 25

He writes from his family home near Vienna. He
apologizes for the disgrace I have suffered and for the
injustice that he has not endured it with me. He tells me
that he loves me more than ever, but says that I should
not come to him, for he suspects he is being followed -
by whom he cannot say. He has instead rented an

apartment in Basel, Switzerland for me and has made arrangements for my confinement there. He gives me the address and hopes that I still love him enough that I might be willing to live there, and though he cannot promise marriage yet, he nevertheless assures me that he will commit himself to my happiness and the happiness of our child.

June 26

I have told Mama and Steely that I will go to Basel as Felix asks. They say that my reputation will be ruined. They say that the family's reputation will be harmed. They say that Edward will be forced to divorce me. They say that Felix will not marry me.

I say that I do not care.

Finally, they ask that I postpone my decision until I have had a chance to think about the repercussions. I agree to wait one month, while preparations are made for my journey to Switzerland

I shall wait no longer.

Basel, Switzerland
September 5

I have arrived after a long journey. Steely travelled with
me as far as Brussels, but now I am alone with Eugenie
as my only companion. It was thought wise that I
assume a new identity, fearing that the Ellenborough
affair, as it is now called in the London social circles,
might travel with me across the English channel,
through Belgium and France to Switzerland. Madame
Einberg is my *nom de guerre*. I have written to my
family, and to Felix, with news of my safe arrival.

I now wait again, for my lover, for the birth of our child,
and for my fate to be decided for me. The irony is not
lost upon me.

September 10

Ordinarily I would be charmed by my new home and
eager to discover the history and culture Basel offers.
However I am reluctant to explore. It was not until
Eugenie convinced me that we visited the Old Town
with its medieval architecture and walked beside the
Rhine. The excursion brightened my spirits

temporarily, but once back home - should I call it that? - I can only hope for a letter now overdue.

September 12

A letter has arrived, but not the one for which I longed.

Instead, my father writes that Edward now seeks a divorce. News of my affair, and my departure from England to bear the child of my lover has now become the talk of London society. A mere formal separation is no longer possible. Papa assures me that he, Edward, and their solicitors will make sure that I am "well provided for," and that I can expect further details concerning "the matter" in the future.

I can feel no regret, only relief. I cannot be married to a man I no longer love.

September 14

Felix has finally written. He tells that he loves and misses me, but that he still believes he is being followed. He has been advised by his family not to visit me later this month as he had hoped. He will instead call on me when he travels for his new assignment at the embassy in Paris later this November, just before the birth of our child. I now must write to tell him of my impending divorce. I fear his reaction to the news and the possible loss of his love.

I am nearly mad with worry, and with loneliness, Marianne.

October 1

I have just spoken with one of my father's solicitors, a Mr. Wigram, who came to Basel to deliver a copy of a "Bill of Divorce" with an explanation of the terms from my father. Although both he and Edward had hoped to keep the divorce a private matter, the law demands that the bill be heard in both Houses of Parliament, if we are both to be allowed to remarry. I am to be divorced on grounds of adultery, though no such grounds can be brought against Edward or the divorce cannot be granted under British law. I will also forfeit custody of my son Charles. In return I am to be given 360 pounds twice a year for the remainder of my life - in addition to a substantial lump sum when the divorce is final. The hearings will begin early next year.

I have no choice but to agree, or I may never be free to marry again.

October 20

I have received two letters today. I cannot say which weighs more on my heart.

The first is from Mama. My extended family, the entire Digby-Coke-Anson clan, has learned the news of my impending divorce. My brothers, like most young men not concerned with romantic intrigue, care little. They are also busy with their own lives. Kenelm has just started university; Edward now pursues a career in the army. My Aunt Anne, true to character, thinks it much ado about nothing. My cousins, as sensible as their mother, seem also unfazed, according to Mama. I, for a moment, think of George and what his reaction might be. I cannot guess. Only Grandpapa and his young wife are angered. King Coke calls me "a foolish girl" who "evidently cares little for her family's reputation." I suppose my favorite granddaughter status is no longer.

Mama also asks whether she should send Steely, or her sister, Jane, to me for the final weeks of my pregnancy. She says she fears for me with only servants for companionship during the birth and my confinement. She also asked whether I want for anything from home that might make the days ahead easier.

The other letter comes from Connaught Place. Edward offers me an allowance for any expenses during my confinement. He also asks whether I might return the green box of the Law family gems, but insists that I keep any other jewelry he gave me during our courtship and marriage. He wishes me well.

Their kindness and concern overwhelms me, Marianne.

October 22

Eugenie dispatched my letters to Mama and Edward earlier today. Painful hours but few words I spent in my replies:

Dearest Mama,

I beg you to forgive me for any distress I may have caused our family. I do hope that my actions have not caused irreparable harm. Please do not think to send Steely or Jane. Eugenie takes such good care with me, and Felix sees that I want for nothing.

I keep you all in my thoughts.

Ever your grateful daughter,

Jane Elizabeth

My dear Edward,

I hope you will believe me when I say I felt myself
utterly unequal to writing to you. I cannot thank you
enough for your kindness but ask you not to think of
making me such an allowance. Indeed it is more than I
can possibly want. I will send back the green box
tomorrow.

Yours,
Janet

October 31

All Hallow's Eve. Pagans believe that on this date the
walls between the worlds of light and dark are thin
enough that spirits can travel from one to the other.

I am possessed by such dark thoughts tonight.

November 2

Dark thoughts turn light, Marianne! Felix writes that he will be here within the week.

November 12

I have been gloriously happy these past few days. With my Prince here I can imagine us as we should be - married and awaiting the birth of our first child. He spoils me dreadfully. We stroll the cobblestone streets of Basel, attend services at Munster Cathedral, share intimate dinners. We sleep together each night, our bodies fit together like spoons - his hand curls over my swollen belly.

November 22

Our child's entry into the world could not have been better timed.

I had awakened two days ago - the day Felix was to leave for Paris - with birth pangs. The poise and grace so typical of Felix was quickly lost upon his realization that I was soon to give birth to his first child. He ran out of the room in a state of undress to fetch Eugenie, only to return a moment later for his dressing gown. More appropriately dressed, he left again to tell her to bring the midwife and nurses to me. He soon returned to comfort me, though his presence hardly did so. He first paced, then stroked my hair while I suffered through another pang. In no time he rushed to the window, asking me what was taking Eugenie so long and paced again. His frantic behaviour ceased only with Eugenie's arrival with the midwife who ordered His Highness from the room.

Less than six hours later, Felix returned to meet his daughter with a crooked smile gone broad. We agreed to name her after his favourite sister. With Matilde in my arms and Felix by my side, I have never known a day so bright.

November 30

Our contentment has come to a sad but inevitable end with Felix's departure for Paris to his new position at the French embassy. He will not return until the Christmas holiday.

For a girl who does not cry I have done quite a lot of it lately.

December 10

I spend my days admiring my rosebud daughter, who I call Didi for no particular reason other than that she seems to enjoy the sound, which I make when I hold her in my arms. The nurses tell me she is a good baby who cries only when hungry or needs changing. I cannot help but think of my poor Charlie who cried so much and whose health was so frail. I so hope he is well.

I try to dismiss such sad thoughts with preparations for the holidays. I must make the apartment as gay as possible for my Prince. I have placed garlands on the mantel and the staircase railing, and a wreath on the door. I have ordered slippers with an Egyptian motif to be made for him, as well as a Malacca wood walking stick topped with gold filigree. I am even trying my hand at sewing a lace bonnet for Didi with the help of dear Eugenie. Now I must wait for him to return to us.

December 26

Our first Christmas together. May I allow myself the thought that many more are to come, Marianne?

He gave me the most beautiful necklace, an amethyst Riviere, and is delighted with his cane and slippers. But most delighted is he with our dear Didi who looks like a Christmas angel in her lace bonnet. He is completely besotted with his little girl. I don't think I have ever experienced such pleasure as I have found in simply looking at the two together.

My only unhappiness is when I think of England.

December 30

Our Christmas holiday ends early with Felix's departure to Vienna to see his family. But the pain of his leaving is diminished by his request that Didi and I move to Paris. He plans to find us an apartment when he returns to his work at the embassy in the new year.

1830

Basel, Switzerland

January 15

Felix has written that he has leased an apartment large
enough for me, Didi, and the servants in the fashionable
district of *Saint-Germain-des-Pres*, while he keeps his
small one near his embassy. He thinks it best we live
apart until the divorce is finalised. I must agree, but I
hate the idea that I am now a kept woman, Marianne.

Nevertheless, I will enjoy being in Paris again. I hope to
rejoin society after my long confinement - though I
doubt the fashionable there will offer invitations to me.
Pshaw! I do not care. I am certain Madame Einberg will
receive many from the creative set, whose company I
infinitely prefer. I understand that Victor Hugo, the
young man I met on my earlier visit to Paris is now the
toast of the City of Light - as it is now called with nearly
every street lighted with gas lamps!

I am eager to start again, Marianne.

Paris, France

January 30

Need I describe the difficulty of travelling with an infant, a lady's maid, wet-nurse, and a nurse-maid? But all the trouble found in travel was lost with the lovely homecoming Felix prepared for Didi and me. Flower bouquets filled every room. How did he ever find them in the dead of winter?

Our new home is located on a cozy side street with a decidedly Bohemian air. Perhaps here I can rediscover my love of books, art, and music. Perhaps here my Prince and I can secure our future.

February 4

Oh Marianne, I have received the most distressing news from Edward at Roehampton. My sweet Charlie has died. What his nurse thought a minor cold quickly deteriorated into pneumonia, so quickly that Edward could not reach Roehampton before his death. My poor boy died all alone.

Edward enclosed a lock of his hair, more gold than my own.

February 5

I have a theory that Death takes the very young so that they need never know that He will take us all.

April 1

And so our farce begins. Lord Ellenborough's Bill of Divorce will be heard by Parliament today. Lady Ellenborough will not be represented. She is, after all, guilty of adultery. It is only his Lordship's guilt, or not, that needs to be determined.

April 3

Only the lurid reports from *The Times* would have the power to break my despondency over Charlie's death. Front page news from London, England is made available here in Paris, France. The most intimate details of my affair are made wretchedly public. Even the sounds of our lovemaking - reported by that vile man, Hepple - did not escape the scrutiny of the press.

My poor family, as well as Felix, must be mortified. I feel such shame and despair.

On my twenty-third birthday.

April 4

Felix is so maddened by the tabloid commentary. He fears for his reputation, for his position at the embassy, for Didi's future. I fear that his family will now never agree to our marriage, even if my divorce is granted.

April 5

Dear God, will it never end? Now my dear Steely has been forced to testify. I suspect Edward and my family had their hands in this decision. Steely's presence will convince the court that the fault in the marriage is all mine, which is essential for the divorce to be granted. I regret I can see the logic in it. But Marianne, my so very proper governess forced to answer such embarrassing questions. Will she ever forgive me?

April 6

Despite the ugliness of the proceedings I can take heart from two incidents. Will Carpenter, my former groom, has been quite evasive in his responses to questions from prying Parliament members, though he drove me to many of my assignments with Felix. I shall have to make sure his loyalty to me is rewarded. And a chivalrous Parliament member, a Mr. Joseph Hume, defended me. He asked, "What is a young lady to do who is neglected by her husband? Is she to wait at home all day long?"

Indeed, what is a young lady to do, Marianne?

April 7

Our bill of divorce, allowing both Edward and I to remarry, has been granted by Parliament. I cannot improve upon the commentary provided by *The Times*:

"Such a result was all but inevitable, since nobody had the courage to take the true ground - the alleged conduct of Lord Ellenborough with respect to other women."

Despite the injustice of it all, I can only feel relief.

April 10

Just when I think that I can be free of my past and that Felix and I can plan for our future, another intrusion occurs. Now, a novel called *The Exclusives* has presented an account of our affair, an account so exaggerated, but still close enough to the reality, that all of London and Paris will most likely see the novelist's fabrications as the truth. This anonymous author even suggests that I have had affairs with *other* men during my romance with my Prince. Whatever will he say when he learns of this fabrication? He is a jealous man, Marianne.

April 14

As I feared Felix has learned of the novel and its lies. He accuses me of being unfaithful - first with George Anson and then with Monsieur Lambeau who acted as my escort when Felix was conducting business in Vienna. I vehemently denied both charges, saying my affair with my cousin was over long before I met him, and that I was with child when the Monsieur escorted me. I asked whether he thought so poorly of me that he would suspect me of infidelity when carrying his child. He refused to answer.

I believe I have learned the reason for Felix's ridiculous accusations from Count Apponyi who paid me a call yesterday. He warned me that there has been gossip concerning Felix's dalliances at Parisian salons with *two* notorious women, Madame Duval and Madame Renaud. It would seem my Prince is employing a tactic known well by any reader of romances - when guilty of infidelity accuse your partner of the same!

Steely writes that London society has taken to calling Felix, Cad - short for his nickname, Cadland - for his treatment of me.

Calais, France

April 28

I fled Paris with Didi to the *Hotel Meurice* in Calais after a dreadful argument with Felix. He claims that he can no longer trust me. I told him that it is *I* that cannot trust *him*, having learned of his romances with the Madames. He said that they were mere flirtations, spurred by my own unfaithfulness.

Clearly, he is as familiar with romantic plot lines as I.

May 7

Mama and Steely have arrived from Forston in an attempt to convince me to leave Felix and return to England with Didi. They argue that I could come home and that after the scandal has died down, I could rebuild my reputation and social standing, possibly even remarry and enjoy a comfortable life made possible by Edward's generous settlement.

I really could not.

May 10

Felix has written. He asks me to return to Paris. He misses Didi and begs that I forgive him.

I do not reply.

Paris, France

May 30

I returned to Paris, unhappy and unmoored.

May 31

Felix, learning of my return, writes, asking whether he might call on me tomorrow. I reluctantly agree.

I must think, Marianne.

June 1

I have given Felix an ultimatum. We must marry, or I shall leave him. He promises to write his family in Vienna that we will marry with their approval or not.

I worry that he promises so willingly.

June 20

The last three weeks have given me some hope. When I hear Felix sing softly to Didi, I hope. When I see his face beside me as we make love, I believe. But those moments do not last long enough to fill the hours without him. I long for more, though fear false hope.

June 27

I have received word from London that King George IV died yesterday. He is succeeded by his brother, William IV. Long live the King.

July 1

I asked Felix whether he had written his family concerning our marriage. He said he had not. He swears that he will do so tomorrow. Of course, he had many reasons for his delay.

I believe only one reason is true. He does not want to marry me.

July 20

Felix has finally received word from Vienna concerning our marriage. Word is not good. As Roman Catholics, they object to his marrying a divorced woman. They object to the scandal caused by my divorce, saying that Felix's career may suffer for it.

I should not be surprised that his role in the divorce and scandal is not mentioned.

July 21

We argue - again.

I ask that we marry by common license within a fortnight.

He refuses, saying that we should give his family time, that our patience will prove the seriousness of our intent.

I say that *my* patience is running thin, that I cannot trust him to honour his commitment.

He replies that it is *me* that cannot be trusted, that it is *my* behaviour that drives a wedge between us.

He leaves and does not return.

July 27

Paris has gone mad. Ordinary Parisians have taken to the streets to protest recent ordinances of King Charles and his ministers. It is as though Paris is undergoing another French Revolution. I tremble at the thought, Marianne. Workers are fighting soldiers in streets, using roof tiles and flower pots, shouting, "Death to the ministers" and "Down with aristocrats." The soldiers fired only warning shots at first, but soon over twenty citizens lie dead in the streets. I fear for Felix's safety, as well our own, though I hope my assumed name, Madame Einberg, will protect us!

July 28

I spent a restless night, though this morning Felix has sent word, assuring me that he is safe, and telling us all to remain at home and answer the door to no one, though he believes that the situation is under the control of the city's garrison and that negotiations are underway. I place trust in his knowledge.

July 29

Negotiations have failed. Royalists have fled, and now the "people's flag" of revolution is flying on buildings across the city. A provisional government has been created. Peace has been restored, though tensions still linger.

July 30

Felix has safely returned to us. He says that it is likely that King Charles will be forced to abdicate the throne in favour of the Duke of Orleans.

He also tells me that he has written to his sister, Matilde, to ask that Didi and I might visit her at her home in Vienna to escape the turmoil in Paris, though his diplomatic obligations will force him to remain in Paris.

Is this not extraordinary, Marianne? I am surprised at the suggestion, but am eager to meet Felix's beloved sister. Perhaps she might soften his family's resistance to our marriage.

I must write to Mama of my safety and of my plans to leave for Vienna.

Vienna, Austria

August 20

My entourage - Eugenie, Didi, her nursemaids - and I have arrived in Vienna, the city of music. Felix has spoken of the city with such fondness that I looked forward to seeing it for myself. In particular, I wished to take coffee in Vienna's oldest coffee house, *Cafe Frauenhuber*, of which he spoke nostalgically. Glittering chandeliers. Red velvet seats. Billiard tables. Card games. The bittersweet smell of cigars and coffee. But of course women are not permitted to enjoy such establishments. No matter. I am certain I will enjoy what else this grand city has to offer.

I must admit I was nervous about meeting Felix's favourite sister and introducing Didi to her namesake. However my fears were unfounded. The Princess could not have been more welcoming, and her resemblance to Felix is uncanny. The same wavy hair, the same crooked smile, the same piercing eyes. Even her gentle voice echoed Felix's, as she spoke of their shared childhood in Bohemia. He alone could calm her girlish

fears and ease the persistent sick headaches she
endures to this day.

So how could she not love her brother's child? She
holds Didi with such delight and affection that I could
not help but envy that womanly instinct with babies
that all women I know seem to possess, except me.

August 22

Today the princess and I tour the old city on foot. With
its Baroque churches and palaces, it is easy to imagine
that we are in Italy, not Austria. I could have walked the
streets for hours, though unfortunately Matilde cannot.
She reveals to me that she tires easily since suffering a
grave fever during her adolescence. Her family and
doctors so feared for her life that marriage and children
were thought too dangerous for her fragile health.

I ask whether she regrets not marrying or having
children. "Not the marrying," she replies.

August 24

Didi, at nine months, is an intrepid explorer. I watch
her antics, as she crawls nimbly across the floor to

Matilde and grasps her gown so that she might pull herself to standing. She fails and falls to the floor with an angry cry.

"Let me call her nurse," I say.

"No, please. I enjoy her so," replies Matilde, as she scoops Didi into her arms.

August 25

"My brother can never marry you," she tells me today. She says what I have heard before but have refused to heed - that my divorce and her brother's Catholic faith will prevent our marriage, and that our continued affair is jeopardizing his diplomatic career. "If it were not for Didi, he would have broken with you months ago," she adds.

"Did Felix ask that you speak to me?"

"Of course, my dear."

How carefully they planned it all.

August 26

She suggests that I take a much needed holiday and offers to keep Didi for as long as I wish, so that I might better enjoy my freedom.

My freedom, Marianne. I must make the difficult choice for me - and for my daughter.

August 29

The Princess has not mentioned her suggestion again. Instead, she watches me, giving me time to consider a future not complicated by the past.

August 31

I have written family friends, the Erskines, in Munich, asking whether I might visit with them. Lord Erskine, a good friend of my grandfather, is the British ambassador there.

Matilde, not surprisingly, is pleased by the news.

The Road to Munich
September 10

I said goodbye to my daughter early this morning. I kissed her sweet face as she slept.

I shall not allow myself to regret my choice. She will be loved, of that I am certain - her future too will be more certain than one I could give her.

I shall now have the freedom that has always eluded me. As the coach-and-four carries Eugenie and me forward, my past recedes - farther and further. The road ahead is open and uncharted.

I begin again.

To Be Continued

Volume Two of Jane Digby's Diary: A Rebel Heart is available in the Kindle store.

A Note About Code

Jane frequently wrote in code in her diaries, perhaps in fear that someone might read her most private thoughts without her permission. I too include short passages in code whenever she reveals something of a truly private or incriminating nature. For the code I chose a Caesar D cipher, the key to which I have included below for those readers who would like to be privy to Jane's most intimate declarations:

D=A
E=B
F=C
G=D
H=E
I=F
J=G
K=H
L=I
M=J
N=K
O=L
P=M
Q=N
R=O
S=P
T=Q
U=R
V=S
W=T
X=U
Y=V
Z=W
A=X
B=Y
C=Z

Author's Note

I suspect most writers of historical fiction have struggled with the distinction between historical fact and historical fiction. I too have struggled with how to best represent the historical Jane with the Jane of my imagination. Much is known about the real Jane, indeed three biographies have been written about her. Some of her correspondence has survived, as well as some of her diaries, though much was lost or perhaps destroyed, by a disapproving descendent it is thought. What else we know of Jane comes from the writings of her contemporaries, who knew her or knew of her. The rest must be filled between the lines, much like crayoning the spaces of a sketch in a coloring book.

I believe I have stayed true to Jane's character, despite my reconstructions of the realities of her life. I have changed dates and chronologies to better suit the demands of a diary format and combined or embellished characters where I thought necessary. I have even created incidents in her life when I thought some justification was needed for her actions. And although I have tried to avoid anachronisms, I also wanted Jane's voice to sound contemporary enough that my readers could imagine her as any young woman, not merely one from 19th century Britain. I am convinced her story is one that can bridge the span of more than a century.

I strived - and will continue to strive - to create the best Jane I can, to do justice to a remarkable woman who led an extraordinary life.

Acknowledgements

First and foremost, I would like to acknowledge three biographies written about Jane Digby that were crucial in my research of her life: *The Odyssey of a Loving Woman* by E.M. Oddie, *Passion's Child* by Margaret Fox Schmidt, and *A Scandalous Life: The Biography of Jane Digby* by Mary S. Lovell. The first biographies are no longer in print, though the Lovell biography is available in print and as an ebook. I highly recommend it for readers who would like to know more about Jane's scandalous life.

In addition, I also recommend *The Wilder Shores of Love* by Lesley Blanch. A compilation of stories about 19th century women who "followed the beckoning Eastern Star," the book includes a biography profile and commentary concerning what led Jane Digby to find her heart and home in Syria.

I would also like to thank the numerous writers whose blogs I visited for research to help me bring to life the customs, locales, and personages of the early 19th century in a textured way. I consulted more than I can mention here, but I would like to acknowledge some of my favorites:

Lisa Graves's *History Witch*
Elena Greene's *History, Heart, and a Touch of Heat...*
Kristen Koster's wonderful blog on Regency minutiae
Mirella Patzer's *History and Women*
Kathryn Kane's *The Regency Redingote*
Mimi Matthews's elegant blog concerning romance, literature, and history
Vic Sanborn's *Jane Austen's World*
Strange Company: A Walk on the Wild Side

I would also like to acknowledge the period miniature of Jane Digby by William Charles Ross that I used as cover art.

And last but not least, I thank my husband, Ken, who acts as my proofreader, editor and sounding board. I love you more than you know.

About the Author

C.R. Hurst, who taught writing and language at a small college in Pennsylvania for over 25 years, retired early and moved to the North Carolina mountains where she lives with her husband and a little black cat named Molly. CR loves the outdoors, reads too much and writes too little. A realist with two feet planted in the 21st century, she nevertheless enjoys escaping into the past with historical fiction. *Jane Digby's Diary* is her first novel.

And one more thing . . .

Independent writers like me need the support of readers like you. If you enjoyed *Jane Digby's Diary*, please leave a review on Goodreads and/or Amazon.

Thank you,
CR

Made in the USA
Las Vegas, NV
17 June 2024

91176608R00132